"You're despicable!"

Nina took a breath and then continued, "You think you can take control of people like you take control of your petty companies. Well...." She turned to glare at him. "I am not for sale, Mr. Lakitos. Just remember that when Jason is around, because if I had to make a choice between you and him, I would choose Jason any day."

"So you are not for sale, heh?" He didn't sound angry, just curious.

Nina sent him a disdainful look. "No. I love Jason!" she announced forcefully. And she did, she told herself desperately. She did! "And as soon as my father is well enough to hear the news, I will be marrying Jason!"

"You will not," Anton Lakitos smoothly drawled, "because you, Miss Lovell, will be marrying me."

MICHELLE REID lives in Cheshire, England, dividing her time between being a full-time housewife and mother, looking after her husband and two teenage daughters and writing. She says her family takes it very well, fending for themselves until she "comes up for air," though she's not sure which they find harder to put up with, being cleaned and polished when she's in a housekeeping mood, or being totally ignored when she's absorbed in writing and tends to forget they're alive! She has a passion for fresh air and exercise, which she gets at the local tennis club.

Books by Michelle Reid

HARLEQUIN PRESENTS
1440—A QUESTION OF PRIDE

HARLEQUIN ROMANCE
2994—EYE OF HEAVEN

Don't miss any of our special offers. Write to us at the following address for information on our newest releases.

Harlequin Reader Service
P.O. Box 1397, Buffalo, NY 14240
Canadian address: P.O. Box 603,
Fort Erie, Ont. L2A 5X3

MICHELLE REID

no way to begin

Harlequin Books

TORONTO • NEW YORK • LONDON
AMSTERDAM • PARIS • SYDNEY • HAMBURG
STOCKHOLM • ATHENS • TOKYO • MILAN
MADRID • WARSAW • BUDAPEST • AUCKLAND

If you purchased this book without a cover you should be aware that this book is stolen property. It was reported as "unsold and destroyed" to the publisher, and neither the author nor the publisher has received any payment for this "stripped book."

Harlequin Presents first edition July 1992
ISBN 0-373-11478-8

Original hardcover edition published in 1991
by Mills & Boon Limited

NO WAY TO BEGIN

Copyright © 1991 by Michelle Reid. All rights reserved.
Except for use in any review, the reproduction or utilization
of this work in whole or in part in any form by any electronic,
mechanical or other means, now known or hereafter invented,
including xerography, photocopying and recording,
or in any information storage or retrieval system, is forbidden without
the permission of the publisher, Harlequin Enterprises Limited,
225 Duncan Mill Road, Don Mills, Ontario, Canada M3B 3K9.

All the characters in this book have no existence outside the
imagination of the author and have no relation whatsoever to
anyone bearing the same name or names. They are not even
distantly inspired by any individual known or unknown to the
author, and all incidents are pure invention.

® are Trademarks registered in the United States Patent and
Trademark Office and in other countries.

Printed in U.S.A.

CHAPTER ONE

IT WAS a dark, dank, filthy night. One of those nights when nothing stirred, nothing but the relentless fall of fine drizzly rain from a low bank of cloud which hung oppressively overhead.

Nina Lovell stood just inside a pair of wrought-iron gates, staring across the shadowed lawns at a white-rendered mansion house. There was some kind of party going on up there. The driveway was packed with cars, and there was light spilling from almost every ground-floor window. The muted sound of music drifted towards her on the damp mizzly air.

She shivered, huddling deeper into her thin summer coat, cold hands clenched inside her coat pockets. Somewhere inside that house, the man she had come here to see was enjoying himself, while several miles away, in a house not dissimilar to this one, lay the victim of his latest *coup*, dying from the horror of it all.

'He can't do it to me, he can't——!' Jonas Lovell had cried out just before a heart attack sent him crumpling to the study floor.

But apparently he could do it, and was about to if he couldn't be stopped. Which was why she had come here tonight. She had come to beg, plead, bargain if necessary. Do whatever it took to relieve her father's stress. Did *he* know about Jonas Lovell's heart attack? And if he did know, didn't he care that in order to swell his own already massive property empire he had crushed another man into the ground?

She despised men like him, and a deep shiver shook her slender frame. Her father did not deserve what was happening to him. His whole life revolved around

5

Lovell's. Take it away from him and he had nothing left to live for.

'He's fretting,' the doctor had told her worriedly. 'Something has to be done to ease his mind, or I'm afraid he may suffer another attack.'

With the misty rain clinging like fine gossamer to the long loose fall of her red-gold hair, Nina started forwards, moving with a strange, ghostly grace along the line of sleek, expensive cars, the spill of light from the house catching at the stark white pallor of her skin as she went. It was gone ten o'clock, and she had hardly moved from her father's bedside for three long days and nights; fatigue was dragging at her limbs, her mind, her aching heart. Only concern for her father and a deep-seated malevolence for the man she had come here to see kept her going, forcing her to place one tired foot in front of the other, pausing only when she reached the deep circular porch supported by two white pillars.

What now? she wondered blankly.

The man she had come to see was throwing a party. Did she simply bang on his front door and demand to see him anyway?

No, she shuddered at the very idea of it. It was bad enough having to come here to beg from him without risking having an audience to watch her do it.

God, she was tired . . .

A pale hand slipped out of her pocket to rub across the heavy press of her brow. The worry that had become her constant companion for the last three terrible days was sapping her ability to think clearly. She wasn't even that certain she was actually standing here—or existing in some kind of misty nightmare which included her father's illness as well as this unwelcome journey.

She wished it could be a dream, she thought heavily as she lowered her hand to stare at the white-painted front door to the house. She would give anything to just wake up and find her father fit and well, and the need to place herself anywhere near the man who owned this house non-existent.

He frightened her. He had from the first moment she had set eyes on him. No one should be allowed to be as powerful as this man was—nor so disturbingly attractive.

Something inside her coiled into a tight ball in the pit of her stomach, then sprang out in a jarring wave of agitation that had her feet scuffling on the black bitumen driveway and her eyes flickering huntedly around her before she found the strength to quell the fear, and return her gaze to the white-painted front door.

It was only then that she noticed how it was standing slightly ajar, and the agitation altered to a tingling glow of excitement as an idea slid unbidden into her head.

Dared she just walk into his house without permission?

The door seemed to have been left open in invitation to any latecomers to his party. Well, she thought cynically, she was late, though not invited.

She had come here to see Anton Lakitos, and see him she would before the night was out. Even if that meant sneaking into his house and hiding away somewhere until she was sure she could get him alone.

Her chin went up, soft mouth setting in a thin line of determination, and she moved slowly forwards, stepping carefully through the narrow gap in the door.

And found herself standing in a deep inner vestibule, the floor beneath her feet ornately tiled in black and white inlaid with gold. Dark red velvet hung across the inner archway, pulled back into two deep drapes by gold tasselled cords. Beyond them was a large square hallway softly lit by oyster-silk-shaded wall-lights that glowed warmly against the oak-panelled walls and richly polished floor. A wide central stairway swept elegantly upwards to a shadowed landing, its shallow treads covered in a thick dark red carpet.

The hall was surprisingly free of people, the several doors leading from it all closed, keeping the sounds of enjoyment to a low level. And, ignoring the way the heavy pump of her heart was telling her that what she was doing was nothing short of criminal, she went forwards, slipping around the curtains to take a fleeting glance to her left and right before making a dash for the stairs, her footsteps light on the polished wood floor, some hazy sense of reason telling her that if she could only make it to the floor above then maybe she could find somewhere up there to wait undetected until the party was over.

With the sense of her own culpability running like pure adrenalin in her veins, she ran up the stairs, only just making it to the top when a door below was opened, and she dropped quickly down behind the polished balustrades just in time to see two men come out of one of the rooms, closing the door behind them.

Anton Lakitos, she saw immediately, confirmation coming with the sudden hectic clamour of her pulses. They, like she, would recognise him anywhere.

Tall, wide-shouldered and powerfully built, Anton Lakitos was the most intimidatingly attractive man she had ever encountered. Everything about him disturbed her deeply, from the way the jet-black sheen of his hair swept smoothly away from the hard-angled shape of his face, to the rigid squareness of his jaw with its inbred tilt of arrogance. His mouth was wide and firm and shockingly sensual. His nose was long and straight, an essential line to his lean-boned face. The face of a man who knew what he was and where he was going in life. A man who had been consistently undermining her composure from the first time—months ago—when their eyes had met in an electrifying clash of the senses. Dark— dark brown eyes, burning into her own with a power that was both terrifying and dangerously hypnotic.

And even while she had mentally backed off from what that look said to her, even as she had given a stunned shake of her head in outright rejection of both him and his messages, she had recognised the rich natural tan of the Mediterranean man. The eyes, the hair, the sheer muscled beauty of his body all screamed 'Italian' at her. Like the elegant cut of his hand-made suit, his shirt, his shoes, his whole manner. She had therefore been surprised to learn later that he was Greek. For he had seemed to suit her idea of a high-born Italian better than the darker, more ruggedly hewn Greek man.

Not a week had passed since that first collision when he hadn't somehow manoeuvred them into the same company. And every time they met he caused that same explosion of feeling inside her, forcing her to back right away from him in sheer self-defence of what it all meant. She didn't trust him—couldn't trust that kind of hot sexual pull. To her, he was a sophisticated man of the world, while she was nothing but a shy and nervous student of music, attending the same lavish functions he attended because her tycoon father demanded it of her.

He'd tried every ploy available to him to get closer to her, coming to stand or sit by her side at any opportunity he got, forcing her to be aware of his presence, of the white-hot static that flashed constantly between them, smiling a little sardonically when she continued to hold herself aloof from him, refusing to leave her father's side or even talk to him if she could get away with it without appearing unforgivably rude. She had rejected every approach he made towards her until, eventually, he'd backed right off and continued his unsettling of her senses from afar, dark eyes burning with a look she could only describe as a 'want'. A hot and hungry, unhidden kind of want, that had kept the colour riding high in her cheeks and her breath locked up tight in her chest for as long as they occupied the same room.

He'd begun to haunt her dreams, and she had begun making excuses not to accompany her father to the places where he might be. 'Don't be stupid, Nina,' old Jonas had snapped out irritably. 'I need you with me, and that's all there is to say about it. Anyway,' he'd gone on testily, 'it's high time you realised that there is more to life than your piano and that damned Jason Hunter!' Poor Jason

had never earned favour in her father's eyes, no matter
how hard he tried. 'And stop being so frosty towards
Anton Lakitos!' he'd added impatiently. 'I've got some
delicate business brewing with him, and I don't want
your cold manner rocking the boat.'

Well, she thought now bitterly, something had certainly rocked the boat, because Anton Lakitos was
threatening to take over her father's company, and poor
Jonas was lying sick to the heart with the horror if it.

'Are you sure, John?'

The sound of that low-pitched and grim-sounding
voice brought her attention clattering back to the two
men standing in the hallway below her.

'Yes, sir,' the other man replied. 'He's waiting to speak
to you on the telephone, right now.'

'Damn,' the Greek muttered, then, 'Damn,' again.
Then, 'OK, John, I'll speak to him in my study.' And
Nina crouched further into the shadows as both men
moved across the hall, parting at a pair of doors which
Anton Lakitos flung open and strode through while the
man called John disappeared towards the back of the
house.

A moment later, Nina heard the muffled tones of a
one-sided conversation. His voice was pitched too low
for her to catch any of the words, but she could hear
enough to know he was receiving bad news. Good, she
thought. I hope one of his rotten deals has fallen through.
I hope he's lost every penny he has!

This might well be her best chance to get him on his
own! she realised on a sudden rush of agitation that had
her jerking upright, only to gasp out painfully when her
cramped leg muscles protested at the sudden movement
after being held in a crouched position for so long.

Wincing, teeth biting down into her bottom lip, her
face so white it looked ashen against the quickly drying
tumble of red-gold hair, she took a step towards the
stairs—only to go completely still again as another door
opened below her.

The sound of music lifted, filling her ears, grating along every nerve-end, making her small teeth clench, gold-tipped lashes flickering as she glanced downwards to see a dark-haired woman leave the room Anton Lakitos had just come from.

Aware that the voice in the study had stopped speaking, Nina watched the woman walk gracefully across the hall. She was beautiful, exquisitely so. Tall, dark and perfectly shaped, she was wearing a sleek bronze silk gown that shimmered in the soft light, moving with the sensual grace of her body.

'Anton?' Her voice was sensual too, like thick cream on honey as she called out softly, 'Where have you got to, darling?'

The enquiry brought her to the threshold of the study, and Nina crouched down low again so she could see further into the room. Anton Lakitos came back into view, a glass of what looked like whisky in his hand.

'Aah...' Nina heard the woman drawl. 'So, you drink alone! You perhaps find your guests tedious company tonight?' Her arms went smoothly around his neck, and Nina felt a surprise shaft of resentment shoot through her. They were lovers, it was obvious!

'A business call, no more,' her host assured her, smiling slightly as he bent to place a light kiss on the woman's lips. 'I was on my way back to you all, Louisa.' He scolded lightly, 'You had no need to come in search of me.'

'But I missed you, darling!' the thick-as-cream voice exclaimed, and she moved closer to him, curving her body into the hard-packed line of his. 'Shall we get rid of them, Anton?' she suggested huskily. 'Send them all away so you and I can——'

'Not tonight, Louisa,' he declined, softening the blow by placing another kiss on her pouting mouth. 'Tonight I have some important business to attend to once everyone has gone.'

'More important to you than me?' she miaowed, batting her long black lashes at him.

Anton Lakitos took a sip from the glass he was holding and firmly detached himself from the clinging woman. 'Go back to the other guests, Louisa. I'll join you all in a moment,' he said, so ruthless about the dismissal that even Nina stiffened.

So did the lovely Louisa, her big eyes widening as he turned his back on her, taking another deep sip at his drink. Then she was giving a haughty toss of her head, the flash of anger in her eyes quite startlingly venomous before she was pinning a sweet smile on her face and stepping close to him again.

'Oh, darling...' she murmured coaxingly, 'don't be cross with Louisa.' Red-tipped fingers did a pretty dance along his shoulder until they reached the tense lines of his jaw where they began stroking caressingly. 'She's sorry if she spoiled your private drinking party.'

Anton shook his head, laughing softly as if in spite of himself at her childishly teasing tone. Some of the tension seemed to seep out of him and his smile was wryly mocking as he turned back to face Louisa. 'You've never been sorry for anything in your whole life, you little minx,' he scolded, hooking an arm around her slender waist to pull her against him. 'If I ask you nicely to go back to my guests, will you go?' he ruefully begged.

The sulky pout became a sensual smile. 'Kiss me properly,' she demanded, 'and I shall promise to do anything you ask of me, anything at all...'

The invitation was blatantly clear. 'Minx,' he murmured again, just before his mouth lowered to cover hers.

Disgusted with what she was seeing, Nina got up, ignoring the nagging protest in her limbs this time as she turned and escaped quickly into the shadows of the upper landing. A strange sickening feeling was erupting in her stomach, a further rejection of everything Anton Lakitos was. The man had no scruples, no morals. He might have spent the last few months lusting after Nina Lovell, but it didn't stop him taking his pleasure wherever else it was offered!

The tiredness she had been struggling with for days now came slamming down on her head again, and, without really thinking what she was doing, she opened the door nearest to her and slipped quietly through it, closing it and leaning wearily back against it with her eyes closed, heart pumping sluggishly in her breast.

What in heaven's name am I doing here? she found herself wondering for the first time since she had started out on this crazy mission.

It only took the sunken grey image of her father lying so gravely ill to remind her. She was here because of him. And on that grim reminder she sucked in a deep steadying breath of air—then went perfectly still as her senses picked up on the subtle masculine scent lingering in the air around her, and her heart gave a violent trip.

This was his room!

She had smelled that scent only minutes ago as he crossed the hallway, the musky fragrance drifting up towards her on the warm air. She had been inhaling the same heady scent every time he came close to her over the last months, been instantly drawn to it, and never quite been able to rid her senses of it since.

Slowly, reluctantly, she opened her eyes.

The room was as dark as the grave, and she shivered, her arms going up to fold across her body in an age-old act of self-protection.

Her coat was wet, she noted absently, the sleeves clinging uncomfortably to her bare arms beneath, and she shrugged it off, holding it clasped tightly in front of her while she gave her eyes time to adjust to the gloom.

Slowly, things began to take shape, dark bulks looming out of the walls: wardrobes, chests, and the squat shape of a couple of easy chairs, one of which was standing beside a rather imposing bed. She managed to make out a window, covered with heavy curtains which were blocking out all hint of light.

Taking a few hesitant steps forwards, she came to another halt halfway across the thick carpet, the silence in the room almost as oppressive as the darkness it embraced. It was like standing in some dense black void; her every sense was screaming out against it.

Her shoulders slumped wearily, the sticky dampness of her clothes and the stifling warmth of the room all helping to fill her with a hazy sense of unreality.

If she weren't feeling so tired, if she weren't so heartsick and worried about her father, if she didn't hate and despise Anton Lakitos as much as she did, then perhaps she would be able to see the humour in getting herself into this crazy situation.

But as it was she could barely think at all.

She would wait here, she decided on a stubborn firming of her quivering jaw. She would wait here until Anton Lakitos came to bed—if he came to bed—and then if he came alone.

If he didn't, then she didn't know what she would do...

God, she was tired...

The carpet beneath her feet muffling any hint of sound, she moved forwards again until her foot made contact with the base of the chair near the bed, and she sank down into it. It was a soft-cushioned velvet easy chair, big and welcoming to her weary body. A yawn caught her by surprise, and she smiled wryly at it as her aching body wilted further into the chair's yielding softness, tired fingers letting go of her damp coat so it fell in a rustling heap to the floor beside the chair, her weary brain filling with a muzzy confusion. She had not slept for three nights. Had hardly moved from the chair beside her father's bed. And his restless voice had droned on and on, mumbling senseless phrases about Lovell's and money and Anton Lakitos until she had been able to stand it no more, and she had leaned over him to ask anxiously, 'What can I do for you, Daddy? What can I do to make you more comfortable?'

'He wants everything,' he had mumbled fretfully. 'You, Lovell's, my self-respect, everything.'

'Who does?' she had cried. 'Tell me, and I'll——'

'Why couldn't you have been a son, Nina?' The age-old complaint had left his lips without his being aware of how much it hurt her. 'This wouldn't have happened if you'd been a son! God——' he choked, becoming agitated again. 'He has to be stopped——' He'd tried to get out of bed, and it had taken all Nina's strength to make him lie back down again. 'He won't be happy until he's stripped me of everything—everything...' he had gasped out as he fell weakly back against the pillows.

'Who won't?' she'd pleaded, frightened, really frightened, hating to see him like this. He was usually such a strong and forceful man, so full of life and sharp shrewd cunning, that she had found it difficult to believe that anyone could hurt him this much.

'Get rid of him, Nina, before he ruins you too,' he'd whispered fiercely. 'The greedy, no good... Get Anton... Stop him!' he had groaned, and at last had told her, without her having to ask again, just who it was who was responsible for doing this to him.

So, here she was, come to stop him. By whatever means she had available to her. Prepared to fight, claw, beg or bleed to do it. But not before she'd told Anton Lakitos what she thought of him face to face. Not until...

No, that wasn't right. Nina rubbed her aching head. You don't attack a man then beg for his mercy. You would get nowhere with those kind of tactics...

Her eyes felt hot and heavy, the pitch darkness filling her with a sense of utter emptiness, so that she couldn't think clearly, as if she weren't really here at all.

Slipping off her shoes, she curled her legs up beneath her and began rubbing at her damp cold toes, surprised to find out that she had come here without even putting on any stockings. She had just left her father's bedside, walked out of the room and down the stairs, then—then what?

She couldn't remember. It hurt to even try. She was here. How, she had no idea, but here she was, she was sure of it.

That last thought brought the wry smile back to her tired mouth. You're losing touch with your mind, Nina, she mocked herself. If you don't watch out, they'll be coming to take you away!

All she had to do now, she told herself firmly, was keep her eyes fixed on the dark shape of the door directly in front of her, and wait—wait . . .

Outside, the rain continued to fall with a silent monotony. Inside the dark room, all was quiet, peaceful. Her head began to droop, her eyelids along with it. Once or twice she managed to jerk herself awake, but eventually, inevitably, she lost the battle with sleep, curling deeper into the softly padded armchair as the minutes ticked away without her actually being aware of them...

Downstairs, the party began to break up. Car doors slamming, people calling out, engines revving, laughter, chatter, then nothing as a quietness settled over the whole house, and still Anton Lakitos did not come to bed.

Hours later, deep into the miserable night, the bedroom door came open and closed again. The muttered curses of a man who wasn't quite in control of his actions sounded in the darkened warmth of the room as he stripped off his clothes and left them to fall in an untidy heap on the floor. He was tired, fed-up, and too full of malt whisky to think further than his waiting bed. The phone call earlier had just about finished off a frustrating few months for him, and all he wanted to do now was sleep, sleep off the whisky and forget all his problems for a while...

Nina came awake with a start, eyes opening wide and bewildered, staring into the pitch blackness with a total disorientation with her surroundings. Something had woken her. What, she couldn't say, but she cried out softly as she jerked into a sitting position, a sense of an unknown fear sending icy shivers down her spine.

'What the——?'

The voice, sounding muffled and slurred, had her coming out of the chair to stand swaying dizzily, her confused mind comparing her surroundings, the muffled curse, and the chair she had been sleeping in, with her father's bedroom where she had spent the best part of the last three days.

'Daddy?' she whispered shakily, groping anxiously for the bed. Knowing she had got something wrong, but unable to work out what.

Without warning, a bulky shape launched itself at her, catching hold of her and dragging her across the bed before she had a chance to react. A moment later and the hard weight of a man's body fell heavily across her own, and in the short space of time it took her to realise just what was happening, she found herself trapped beneath the very naked body of Anton Lakitos.

'Well, well, well, what do we have here?' he murmured huskily, two hands pinning her shoulders to the bed, his warm breath fanning her face, smelling strongly of whisky as he peered at her through the inky blackness. 'Witch or angel?' he idly mused, seeming not in the least bit concerned about finding a strange woman in his bedroom! 'Or maybe a sprightly nymph sent by the gods to soothe this weary mortal's soul!'

'No!' she cried, appalled to hear her own voice leave her with hardly any volume at all. His husky intimation was so obvious that she thrust her hands against his shoulders, gasping as the sleek, smooth heat of his skin confirmed his naked state. 'No!' she choked again, 'Get your hands off me, you——'

'Tut, tut, tut,' he scolded, a long, incredibly sensitive finger coming out to tap her scorching cheek. 'This is my dream,' he announced. 'And I like my nymphs willing, not naughty. Well, maybe a little naughty,' he then amended on a husky little laugh.

He was drunk, she realised with horror. Slewed out of his tiny mind! He thought he was dreaming, when the stupid man had her...

'Let me go!' she spat, pained to find the volume lost in the tight pressure of her throat again. She hit out at him with her fists, cursing thickly to herself when he only laughed and caught her flailing hands, holding them fast in one of his own, pressing them firmly to the mattress above her head.

'Naughty nymph,' he scolded. 'I shall have to silence that pretty mouth with kisses.'

And he did. To Nina's horror, to her utter consternation, his mouth came warm and possessive on top of her own. She stared up at him through the terrible blackness, breath suspended, pulses hammering out of control as she experienced the shock sensation of heated pleasure rushing through her. Then she began to struggle in real earnest, wriggling and twisting beneath him in a frantic attempt to escape the shocking sensuality of his imprisoning mouth.

His, 'Mmm,' of pleasure had her going instantly still beneath him, shock sending blushes to every corner of her tingling flesh when she realised just what her struggles were doing to him.

God, what am I going to do now? she wondered desperately. The man was lost in a drunken stupor! If she woke him up, he could well turn nasty. If she let him go on believing he was dreaming, the consequences could be far more damning.

'Please...' she whispered pleadingly.

'Oh, yes...' he sighed, and the mouth on hers increased its pressure, tasting her, filling her with a peculiar sense of weakness that completely overrode everything else as her own lips began to part—she felt them go with a sense of bewildered horror, yet was unable to stop herself responding. His tongue touched her teeth, then the inner receptiveness of her lips, gently urging her to open further to him. A groan wavered in her throat, a desperate plea for sanity in this insane situation, then he got his own way without her being able to stop him, as her teeth parted of their own volition, and explosions went off in her head.

A hot and naked desire flicked like fire right through her. Shock, the buffeting darkness, her real hatred of this man, all culminated to fling her into a vortex of violent feeling. She wanted to scratch, kick, scream, bite! Yet her body was arching invitingly beneath his, her mouth moving sensually with his own, luring him on, even while she wanted to reject the whole sordid scene.

She was suffocating in her own responses, the breath coming from her body in short tight gasps of arousal. The fight going on inside her head was in no way strong enough to combat the feelings he was so easily awakening in her. He was big and strong, his slick smooth skin an added complication as he moved intimately against her, the heat of him awakening senses inside her she hadn't even known she possessed! The weight of him, the sheer maleness of him, touch, taste, smell, everything backing up to work against her. And the darkness, that terrible disorientating darkness, filling her with a sense of unreality that allowed her to give in to her own desperate bodily yearnings.

'My God, you're sweet.' He was trembling as he moved away a little, his breath a shivering rasp of desire that helped keep her lost in her strange passive limbo. Her hands were released, fingers fluttering as his own ran feather-light over the wild fall of her hair, brushing against her hot cheeks, finding the quivering corners of her mouth to retrace the kiss-swollen contours as though he were a blind man trying to build a picture.

Was he still asleep? She couldn't tell. She couldn't tell anything any more. He began kissing her face, light, warm, tantalising kisses that lifted the fine sensitive hairs on her skin as he brushed her temples, her fluttering lashes, her cheeks, her nose, and finally the soft quivering corner of her mouth where his fingers had just caressed. His hands slipped beneath her, lifting her mouth to the hungry heat of the kiss. Dizzy with confusion, pleasure, fear, and a hundred and one other sensations she didn't dare label, Nina felt his fingers move to the tiny buttons on her blouse, and, as her traitorous breasts began to swell in aching anticipation of his touch, at last she came alive on a horrified explosion of everything.

With a violent thrust, she pushed him off her, taking him by surprise enough to send him rolling back against the pillows. There was a startled moment when neither moved, then she was scrambling up and off the bed, gasping, choking on a build-up of strangled sobs, her only thought to get away from here before he issued the final insult to the Lovell family by taking her without even being aware he had done it!

'Who are you?' he rasped out thickly from the darkness.

Nina went perfectly still, her heart hammering beneath the hectic heave of her breasts, teeth biting down hard on her trembing bottom lip, eyes wide and stinging with wretched tears, her voice locked inside her throat, unable to answer—not wanting to answer.

There was another short pause when no one moved, the silence filling with a terrible foreboding on both sides, then Nina heard the sound of movement, as though he was stretching across the bed to drag something towards him, and she exploded into action again, bending down to search the floor for her shoes, her hair tumbling all over her face to get in her way, irritating her, sending her temperature gauge shooting high as panic completely engulfed her.

She found one shoe, her fingers trembling as they closed around the soft leather sole at the same time as a hand came gently on to her shoulder—and all hell broke loose inside her. She rose up, turning on the balls of her bare feet, and lashed out blindly at the dark bulk looming so terrifyingly close!

CHAPTER TWO

NINA stood stricken into stillness as the dark bulk on the bed gave a pained grunt and jerked violently in reaction.

Then an awful silence settled over the room when nothing moved, nothing but the slow lowering of her hand where the shoe with its lethal-tipped heel still hung between limp, lifeless fingers. And that weird sense of unreality swept over her once again, trapping her in the centre of her own crazy nightmare.

'You stupid bitch!' The violent hiss of words was preceded only fractionally by the full weight of his body landing against her own, sending them both tumbling to the floor with enough force to push the air right out of her lungs. He was breathing like a marathon runner, heaving in deep, noisy gasps of air as he struggled not to completely crush her beneath his own weight.

'You stupid, crazy bitch!' he choked again, wrenching the guilty shoe from her hand and hurling it across the room.

Keeping a painful grip on her shoulders, he dragged himself to his feet, yanking her up with him until they both stood swaying in the nullifying fall-out from their mutual violence.

'You damned stupid fool! What the hell were you trying to do to me?'

Her head came up, drawn by the hoarse thickness of his voice, by the tremors she could feel shaking him. Her hair was all over her face, increasing the sense of nightmare. She couldn't speak, was too shocked by her own violence to think, so she just stood there, staring at him through the thick curtain of hair, her mind a total blank.

He gave her another shake, his fingers biting into the tender flesh of her upper arms as he sent her unruly hair flying out around them so it clung to the clammy surface of his contorted face. A muttered curse had him dragging the fine long strands away, tugging the thick pelt back from her face with a cruel fist so he could thrust his own darkly furious one up to hers.

'Answer me, you crazy bitch!' he snarled when she still just stood there, silent and numb. 'Why the hell are you here in my house? In my room? Trying to put my brains in with a damned stiletto?' Another shake brought her blisteringly alive at last.

'Take your hands off me!' she snarled right back. 'Don't you dare hurt me!'

'Hurt you?' he choked in utter incredulity. 'I ought to beat the life out of you, you stupid, crazy bitch!'

He seemed stuck on what else to call her. His fingers were still biting harshly into her, his teeth, pure white and sharply etched in the consuming darkness, were displaying a fury so palpable she could almost taste it.

Nina threw back her head, defiance in every line of her trembling frame. Blue eyes blazed at thunderous black. 'I hate you, Anton Lakitos!' she spat at him. 'I despise the very sight of you!'

He growled something deep inside his throat, the last threads of his control giving way as he dragged her roughly across the room and slammed her back against the door, ignoring her startled cry as he pressed a muscled arm across her throat, forcing her head back. Her chin was pushed high, and his hand curved tightly over one of her trembling shoulders. She could feel his harsh breath against her face, warm and tormentingly flavoured with whisky, stimulating senses that had been rudely woken only moments ago in the pitch-black frenzy on his bed.

Then he reached out to touch a switch, and Nina squeezed her eyes tight shut against the sudden searing crash of light to her retina. And with her heart thundering against her ribs, she stood, tensed and ready for what had to come next.

It came. 'My God...' The breath left his body on a stunned rush of air. 'Nina Lovell!' he gasped.

Her eyes flicked open, bitter blue arrowing directly on to astonished black. 'Yes!' she confirmed on a contemptuous hiss. 'And you're the heartless swine who is trying to steal my father's company away from him!'

'I'm——?' The black eyes widened, expression revealing utter bewilderment for a moment, before he closed it out on a tight mask of withdrawal. No guilt, no remorse evident anywhere on his hard-boned face as he continued to hold her bitter gaze steady. Then his arm dropped away from her throat. 'I was right,' he muttered grimly. 'You are crazy.'

Nina wilted against the door, the tremors attacking her body making it impossible for her to stand without its support. She could still feel his touch burning on her skin, still taste his kisses on her hot, dry lips, and she dropped her eyes from his, then swallowed thickly when she found herself staring at the pulse point pounding in his throat where beads of sweat glimmered like jewels against his taut brown skin. Crisp hair curled in thick profusion around the rolled-back collar of his dark brown robe—a robe he must have been pulling on when the panic hit her. His powerful chest was heaving in line with the deep gulps of air he was having to drag into his lungs to maintain some control over his temper.

An insidious heat began curling its way through her, its origins so shamefully obvious that she shuddered, a trembling hand coming up to cover her mouth as a wholly appalling desire to place her lips against that gleaming throat shook her to the very core.

In the relative safety of a room full of people, this man had frightened her, but here, with the heated intimacy of what they had so recently shared still raging in her blood, she was experiencing something beyond fear, more a raw dread of her own deeply disturbing desire for this man.

A strained smile touched her mouth. Perhaps he was right, and she was crazy. Only a mindless lunatic would stand here, literally shaking with a need to be possessed by her worst enemy!

He saw the smile and didn't like it. On a sound that came very close to a constrained choke, he grabbed her chin and pushed it up so he could glare at her, eyes so black they seemed bottomless. Black holes for any crazy bitch to fall into.

'You find all of this amusing, do you?' he bit out furiously. 'The fact that I could be lying on that bed right now, bleeding to death, doesn't touch your conscience at all?'

Her gaze flicked over the tense brown skin gleaming healthily back at her. She couldn't see any mark that said she'd actually wounded him. 'I'm—sorry,' she mumbled inadequately.

'Sorry?' he choked. 'You break into my home. Lie in wait for me in my own bedroom. Try to seduce me— then go at me with a damned stiletto!'

'I did not try to seduce you!' she hotly denied, trying to pull away from his biting grip on her chin, but he wouldn't let her, the violence they were both generating almost splitting atoms in the air around them. 'You were drunk!' she accused. 'Too drunk to even know if you were dreaming or not!'

'And what's your excuse?' he derided cynically, bringing the whole shameful episode tumbling down around her, 'No, my dear sweet *nymph*,' he taunted witheringly, 'I wasn't so drunk that I didn't know what a receptive little thing I had clinging like a limpet beneath me!'

'God, you make me sick!' she choked.

'And you, Miss Lovell, make me very—very angry. 'Now...' he made an attempt to get a rein on all the emotions clamouring between them. 'I want to know what the hell you are doing here, and I want to know now, so start talking!'

Nina sucked in a shaky breath, her senses shattered into a million fragments. It was a nightmare, she decided dazedly, just an awful crazy nightmare...

'Talk!' he barked.

No nightmare, not unless you class the last three days as one long waking nightmare, she thought on a shuddering wince as her mind went winging off to that awful moment it had all begun when she had heard her father shouting at this man down the telephone. 'And you can keep your greedy hands off my daughter as well as my company!' had been the final explosion. 'Neither are for the likes of you!'

That, she knew now, had been the moment her father had signed his own death-warrant. You just didn't insult a man like Anton Lakitos and expect to get away with it. Whatever the Greek had answered in return, she didn't know, but when she had rushed into the room after hearing the receiver being replaced with a resounding crash, she had known it must have been catastrophic, because his face had been wiped clean of every vestige of colour. 'He can't do it to me!' he had choked out breathlessly. 'He can't——!' Then the pain had creased his face, and she had had to stand there, watching in horror as he crumpled, clutching at his chest, to the floor.

'The day you had that bitter row with my father, he had a heart attack,' she whispered thickly, anger diminished on a sudden wave of despair.

His black brows drew together in a puzzled frown, and Nina sighed impatiently, further disgusted by this man who couldn't even recall the moment he had caused another man to break apart in horror. 'Three days ago!' she snapped out bitterly, as if talking to an imbecile. 'My father had a heart attack three days ago!'

The frown remained in place, the puzzlement. 'So I found out this evening,' he informed her grimly.

'You didn't know before?' Her head came up, disbelief in the haunted turbulence of her blue eyes.

He shook his head, holding that look. 'I've been away,' he explained. 'I only got back this evening—though what the hell that has to do with any of this, I have no idea...'

He was darker skinned than she'd thought him to be. Taller too, close up, and broader, more—more everything. She dropped her eyes from his again, staring at the way her fingers fumbled with the buttons of her pale blue blouse. A blouse she had put on this morning without any thought to what it looked like, her only concern to shower, change her clothes and get back to her father.

'Since then, I've had to listen to him going on and on about you!' she continued wretchedly. 'Listen to his restless mumblings, w-watch him fade slowly further away f-from me with each new curse he sends you!' She sucked in a deep breath, bitter derision in every line of her tired young face. 'I wanted you to know that, Mr Lakitos. I wanted you to know the results your greed has on your victims. And that is why I'm here tonight,' she finished thickly. 'To tell you that no matter how other people may believe your Midas touch deserves respect, I abhor you! You and your kind make me sick!'

'Thank you.' His dark head dipped in a parody of acknowledgement for every insult she had thrown at him. 'And it was worth leaving your father's sick-bed to impart all of this.' Not a question, but a grim observation of fact. Then he cleverly brought the whole shameful episode into perspective by adding drily, 'Including risking your innocence, it seems.'

'My innocence—or lack of it,' she instantly flared, 'has nothing to do with this!'

'It hasn't?' The dark head tilted to one side, narrowed eyes touching hypersensitive nerve-ends as they ran glitteringly over her. 'I would say it has everything to do with it.' A smile touched his hard mouth, but it was a bleak, uncomfortable thing which stood miles away from humour. 'Anything else you would like to...' he flung out a mocking hand '...get off your chest before we put an end to this—highly informative evening?'

The sarcasm made her cringe, but her chin came up bravely. 'Yes,' she admitted. 'I came here tonight to ask...' It stuck in her throat, and she had to swallow before she could go on. 'To—ask you not to do it to him!'

'Oh?' He didn't sound very receptive, in fact he sounded downright unreceptive, his expression unmoved, eyes grimly implacable.

Nina shifted uneasily. 'Stop trying to make this harder for me than it already is!' she muttered irritably, all too aware that she had made a terrible mess of the whole thing. 'You must surely know what you are without my opinion having shocked you much. OK, so you're angry because I sneaked into your house and tried to hit you, but——'

'Tried?' The black fury was suddenly firing sparks at her all over again. 'A fraction of an inch, Miss Lovell,' he rasped, tugging at the roll-neck collar of his robe and thrusting his left shoulder up to her face. 'That's all, and the steel tip of your shoe would have sunk neatly into the main artery! Are you sorry it did not?'

For the first time he sounded Greek, harshly guttural and shiveringly Greek. Nina swallowed, the pink tip of her tongue tracing the heart-shaped outline of her mouth as she forced herself to look at the ugly red mark slicing across the beautiful dark skin where corded neck met muscled shoulder. It was already beginning to swell around the bruised tear where her shoe heel had cut into the skin. 'I...' Words died in her throat, and she had to drag in a shaky breath to make herself speak. 'I'm sorry,' she mumbled. 'I...' Guilt darkened the blue of her eyes, and, without her actually knowing she was doing it, her hand fluttered up to touch the angry mark with the trembling pad of one finger.

He jerked in response, his own hand coming up to capture hers, fingers tangling, his strong and dark, hers so fine-boned and pale that they looked like delicate porcelain against his. Then the brown of his eyes deepened into a hot dense blackness, and Nina went perfectly still. He was going to kiss her again, she knew it.

Her trembling lips parted. His chest expanded on a harsh intake of air, and her precarious world went topsy-turvy again as their mouths moved to meet in a hungry collision that sent everything else flying.

'God!' It was he who broke the burning contact, dragging himself away from her in angry disgust. 'What are you?' he bit out hoarsely. 'Some kind of sex-starved siren?' Nina bowed her head, shaking the long red curtain of hair. The blood was pounding in her veins with a need so strong she was shaken by it, utterly shamed. 'Damn and blast it, you stupid fool!' he exploded force-fully. 'Have you any idea just what you're inviting here?'

'Mr Lakitos, please listen to me.' She came away from the door to stand trembling in anxious appeal. 'I didn't mean any of this to happen! I—I came here tonight simply to talk to you! About my father—about his illness and—and his distress! I wanted to beg you to help me!' she cried, when he spun the rigid length of his back on her.

'By sneaking into my house?' he growled. 'By throwing insults at me? By trying to put me in my grave before your father was there?' Broad shoulders lifted and fell on an angry breath, his hands thrusting into the deep brown pockets of his robe.

'I—I'm sorry,' she said again. 'I'd fallen asleep in the chair and—and you frightened me...' Small teeth pressing into her trembling bottom lip, she walked for-wards, laying a tentative hand on his arm. 'I lashed out instinctively, I...' It was her turn to suck in a deep breath, the pressure in her lungs so great she felt they might explode soon. 'I w-was at my wit's end when I came here tonight. My father has been lying there for days, restless, mumbling incoherently about his company, money—you,' she told him wretchedly. 'In the end, I couldn't stand it any more!' she cried. 'The doctors are worried that he'll have another attack, and I wanted to ease his restless mind! I—I asked him what was worrying him, w-what I could do to help.' An anguished sob broke from her, and he turned around to view the effects her terrible vigil had wreaked on her pale young face. 'He needs Lovell's, Mr Lakitos,' she finished thickly. 'He has nothing to live for without Lovell's.'

'He has you,' Anton Lakitos said gruffly, glinting eyes hooded by thick black lashes. 'Surely, you are enough to make any man want to live.'

Her smile was pure self-derision. 'I am not a son,' she cynically pointed out. 'You, being Greek, should know exactly what I mean by that.'

'Then you must be crazier than I imagined you to be, if you don't know how much your father cares for you.'

Nina lifted her eyes to stare at him, surprised by the depth of rough-voiced sincerity he'd put into that last statement. And, instantly it was back again, that stinging, stifling, drumming pulse of attraction, glowing in his blackened gaze, throbbing in the space between them, driving the breath from her body and bringing her hand up to cover her lips in horrified recognition of what was charging between them.

Then everything was shifting again, the conflict of emotions swerving from that violent flow of passion to an eruption of anger so unexpected that Nina cried out as he grabbed her wrist in a biting grip.

'What's this?' he bit out harshly, dragging her hand away from her face to dangle her fingers in front of her anxious face. 'What in God's name is this?'

The fingers shook, the bright sparkle of a single diamond glinting accusingly at her.

Nina quaked. 'It—it's a ring,' she breathed.

'I can see it is a damned ring!' he snapped. 'What I want to know is who put it there?'

'My—my fiancé,' she whispered, going pale as a picture of Jason's handsome face leapt up to haunt her. She hadn't given Jason a single thought until that moment! The ring had only been placed on her finger the night before, urged on her by an anxious Jason who wanted her to feel secure in the event of the worst happening to her father.

'Your fiancé,' he repeated, drawing the word out in soft and crushing sarcasm. 'And the name of this—very lucky young man?' he demanded tightly.

'I—Jason,' she stammered thickly, as aware as the man standing in front of her that she had betrayed Jason tonight. 'Jason Hunter.'

'God in heaven.' He threw her hand aside, and Nina caught hold of it with her other one as once again he spun away from her. 'No wonder old Jonas is going——' He stopped himself in mid-sentence, spinning back to face her, eyes narrowed and sharply assessing. 'Jonas does know about this, I presume?' he asked grimly.

'I...' Nina bit down hard on her bottom lip, then shook her head in answer, a new kind of guilt deepening the blue in her eyes. No, she hadn't told her father.

'You know how upset he'll get,' Jason had said, and his smile had been all self-mockery. He knew as well as she did that old Jonas would never accept him as his son-in-law. 'But, at this moment, my concern is for you, not your father's crazy aversion to me. You need the comfort of knowing someone cares about you if—if the worst happens.' And, weakly, she'd given in, too tired to think clearly, and too in need of that comfort he offered to think of refusing it as she should have done.

'Get out of here, Miss Lovell.' The hard, flat tone in his voice made her wince. Anton Lakitos was looking at her through hard, contemptuous eyes. 'Go on, get the hell out of here before I call the police and have you arrested for breaking into my home.'

'Do it!' she instantly flared, angered by his dismissive tone—or maybe because she knew she deserved his contempt. Whatever, she came back spitting, 'Call the police, and I'll tell them how you tried to rape me!'

His eyes flashed coldly. 'Don't make the silly mistake of challenging me,' he grimly warned. 'Or you may find that you have bitten off more than you can chew! Rape, Miss Lovell,' he continued witheringly, 'does not leave the victim panting for more of the same!'

He cynically watched all the colour drain from her face, the ruthless truth of his taunt holding her locked in the horror of her own making.

'Go home,' he repeated grimly. 'Get out of my room, out of my house, and out, Miss Lovell, of my damned life!' Hard eyes sliced her in two where she stood. 'Get back to where you belong, at your father's bedside, in your fiancé's waiting arms, and seek your sexual solace there! But do it now, before I change my mind and take you back to that bed over there to enjoy what you were so recently eager to give me!'

'I wish I hadn't missed with my shoe!' she choked out woundedly.

'Get out!' he shouted. And all at once his control snapped, the harsh mask slipping from his dark face to reveal the rawly angry man.

Without waiting for her to move, he grabbed her arm and swung her back towards the door, flinging it open so it banged back against the wall behind it. Then he was dragging her along the half-lit landing, down the stairs and across the hall to the velvet-draped vestibule.

The cold air hit her flushed face as he opened the front door. Without a single word, he shoved her outside, and she had barely steadied from her inelegant exit before the door had closed firmly behind her.

It was still raining, the steady drizzle falling from the sky to cover everything in a fine veil of silver mist. Nina stared out across the darkened spread of lawn to where a line of tall trees stood quiet and still, tinged purple by the slowly lightening sky. There was a sense of unreality about everything, including herself as she hovered there.

A cold shiver sent her arms wrapping around her body, icy fingers curling around the bare flesh of her arms where the short-sleeved style of her blouse left her flesh vulnerable to the dank, cold chill. Feeling thankfully numb, she stepped out of the porch, the fine rain sheathing her as she walked, her bare feet sinking in the soft spongy grass as she crossed the lawn and then went out through the wrought-iron gates, pausing then to look to her left and her right, wondering vaguely how she had got here.

Taxi, she recalled. She hadn't felt fit enough to drive herself and had come here by taxi. A pale hand lifted to her throbbing brow.

How tired she was. So tired she could sink down here on the cold, wet pavement and sleep, sleep forever. A tremor shook her, deep and cruelly felt, and she turned to the left, bare feet making no sound on the damp, cold pavement as she went.

Within minutes she was drenched to the bone, her slender frame racked with intermittent shudders, the chill seeming to strike from inside out rather than the other way around.

What kind of madness had driven her to come here tonight? she wondered despairingly, covering her eyes with a hand where the tears she had been holding back for a long time were threatening to fall at last.

All she'd seemed to see when she had left her father had been the dark, handsome face of Anton Lakitos smiling at her as he had done so often, offering her a promise of such raw and burning passion that she'd had to stand aloof from it or go up in flames with him. She'd wanted to wipe that smile off his face! Wanted to hurt him as much as he was hurting her! And, she admitted to herself, see if the desire glowing in those devil-black eyes gave her any power over him at all—enough, maybe, to extract some mercy from the man?

It hadn't. She had made an absolute mess of everything, done nothing to help her father, betrayed Jason, and, in the end, she concluded wearily, betrayed herself.

'Oh, God,' she choked, ashamed, bitterly regretting the whole mad night.

It was then that she became aware of a car, crawling slowly up behind her, and she stiffened, a new dread trickling icily down her spine. This was all she needed, a kerb-crawler believing she was a...

Her head twisted sharply as a silver Mercedes drew up close beside her, fumes belching out of the exhaust pipe to mingle with the mizzly mist, and her heart stopped dead in her chest.

The driver's door came open, and Anton Lakitos stepped on to the road, leaving the door swinging wide as he stepped around the car bonnet to open the passenger door.

'Get in,' he said.

Nina stood there, so totally used up inside that she just stared blankly at him. He was dressed, looking completely different in a thick navy sweater and stone-coloured casual trousers. His face wore a mask of grim calm, eyes telling her nothing.

'Get in, Nina,' he repeated quietly. 'I'll take you home.'

Something...the slight softening of his tone, or the brief glimpse of pity she saw in his eyes, or maybe it was just the simple fact that, even after everything, he could not live with himself by allowing her to walk away in the state she was in...whatever, it was enough to crack wide open the control she had been exerting on herself, and her pale face crumpled, chin lowering to her chest as the deep sobs came, and there, in the colourless quiet of the early morning, she experienced the ultimate humiliation, her own emotional collapse in front of this man.

His arm came gently around her shoulders, and, without a word, he guided her over to the car and saw her seated inside, squatting down beside her to personally deal with the seatbelt and flick a car rug over her cold, wet legs. The car door closed with a quiet click, and a moment later he was seated beside her, setting the car into smooth, quiet motion.

They drove in a silence broken only by the sounds of her soft crying, the car's efficient heater trying its best to penetrate the chill of her body. After a while, he leaned across her to twitch open the door to the glove compartment, eyes kept firmly on the road ahead while he rummaged around until he came out with a handkerchief which he dropped into her lap before straightening up again.

'Nina...' he began huskily, once she seemed to have gathered some control over herself. 'We have to——'

Whatever he'd been about to say was cut off as he swerved the car to avoid hitting a big black cat that ran right in front of them. Nina was thrown against his shoulder, and he put out a hand to steady her. His touch burned right into her skin, shocking her into stillness, the brief, wry smile he turned on her telling her that he had experienced the same thing.

'Good luck or bad luck in England?' he quizzed, bringing her eyes flicking warily up to clash with his. He was smiling. 'A black cat crossing one's path means different things in different parts of the world,' he explained the question. 'In Greece, it is a sign of good fortune, but then...' he gave a rueful shrug '...the Greeks are renowned for the love of lucky omens, even if it means altering the fable to suit their needs.'

'You don't sound very Greek,' she observed huskily, shaking with a different emotion now.

Another shrug brought her gaze back to study him. He sat long and lean and lithe in the seat beside her. There wasn't a spare ounce of flesh on him anywhere, yet he exuded a daunting power, the muscled firmness of his body too obvious to be masked. He was a man of disturbing masculinity and her stomach coiled so tightly in response that she had to look quickly away.

'I've lived most of my life in different parts of the world,' he informed her, driving the car with the smooth precision of one who was at ease with power. 'My late father was a member of the diplomatic service, and throughout my formative years I learned to speak all of the most necessary languages quite fluently. English comes the easiest because I was educated here.'

'Black cats are good luck,' Nina stated suddenly and, even as she said it, knew she was taking a leaf out of a Greek book, and turning the superstition to suit herself.

'Then perhaps we will be saved,' he smiled. She could sense his gaze on her. 'Or perhaps not,' he then added drily, and that shocking pulse of awareness came back again, the remnants of what they had shared in the pitch darkness earlier, weaving itself into the air around them, confirming all those feelings she had refused to accept before tonight, forcing her now to recognise her own uncontrollable attraction to this man. He knew it too, Nina could tell by the quick, assessing glances he was giving her. He wanted her, had wanted her from the first moment he had ever set eyes on her, and all she had achieved tonight was letting him see that she was vulnerable to him. He wouldn't let an opportunity like this pass. He wasn't the kind of man who backed off when he saw victory within his grasp.

She shivered, turning her face away from him so he couldn't see the apprehension in her gaze.

'Cold?' he asked. 'I have your coat and shoes in the back of the car, but they are so damp I don't think they would be of much use to you.'

'I'm—all right,' she assured him thickly, and they finished the rest of the journey in silence.

It was the sway of the car as it turned into the driveway that brought her gaze jerking forwards, and the breath left her lungs on a shaky sigh when she recognised her own home.

Tell-tale lights glinted from cracks in the curtains, telling her that no one had gone to bed. She must have left without telling anyone she was going. She couldn't remember. An amnesia born of physical and mental exhaustion had left great gaps in her memory.

She wished she could blank out the events that had taken place since, but she couldn't; they lived sharp and clear in the forefront of her mind, reminding her of what a fool she had been—the stupid, crazy fool, Anton Lakitos had called her.

The silver Mercedes drew to a stop behind another car, and Nina's heart sank. 'The doctor is here,' she said flatly. 'My father must be worse.'

The man beside her turned, shifting in his seat until he was facing her, the movement disturbing the warm air inside the car, and Nina inhaled that clean, musky-scented smell of him, her foolish senses lurching out to grab at it.

'Will you be all right?' he asked quietly.

She didn't answer. What would be the use? She could say yes, she'd be fine, but it wouldn't be the truth. She was suffering from a real dread of finding out what had happened in her absence, of facing the curious looks, the questions, and, inevitably, the truth about her actions tonight.

'God,' she whispered, burying her face in her hands. 'I don't want to go in there.'

'I am coming in with you,' he said firmly.

'No.' She pulled her hands down and fumbled for the door handle, stunned by the way her heart leapt at the offer.

'Yes,' he insisted. 'You can't face them alone. Not in the state you are in. You asked me for my help, and the only way I can give it is by coming inside with you.'

'But...' Now she had it, Nina was no longer sure she wanted his help. Her eyes clouded on her own confusion, and he laid a gentle hand on her shoulder.

'No buts,' he said. 'It's too late now, anyway, the door to your home has just opened and a rather handsome though very aggressive young man has appeared in the doorway.'

'Jason,' Nina noted dully.

'Ah,' drawled the man beside her, and something hard entered his eyes. 'The—affianced. Wait there,' she was told, then he was climbing out of the car and striding around the smooth silver bonnet and opening the passenger door.

CHAPTER THREE

ANTON'S grip on Nina's arm was firm as he helped her out of the car, and she needed it. She was shaking so badly she didn't think she could support herself alone.

'Nina!' Jason stood in the open doorway, looking as though he'd spent the night tearing his hair out worrying about her, and her heart twisted guiltily. 'Where the hell have you been? Have you any idea of the trouble you've put us all to?'

'Hello, Jason,' she answered quietly, her eyes not quite managing to meet the angry concern in his, wondering how the hell she was going to explain tonight's escapade away, and not sure she wanted to even try.

She gave a tug at her arm, but Anton refused to let go of her, guiding her up the steps towards Jason as though he were delivering a rather recalcitrant child back home. Nina felt like a child. A silly, stupid, burdensome child who deserved a good slapping for what she had done tonight.

'You've been gone all night!' Jason's angry voice jarred on her frayed nerves. 'Sadie's been going out of her mind! So have I for that matter! God,' he gasped, 'just look at the state of you!'

Her free hand lifted shakily to her untidy hair. Eyes fixed on her feet where her bare toes were curling in on themselves in shame.

'What the hell got into you—just taking off like that?'

'Nina has been with me,' a deep voice put in smoothly.

'And who the hell are you?' Jason's tone bordered on the downright rude.

'Th-this is Mr Lakitos, Jason,' Nina put in quickly, not liking the way both men were sizing each other up. 'I h-had to see him about——'

'You are Anton Lakitos?' Silver eyes sharpened, flicking narrowly from one face to the other, and Nina cringed inwardly, knowing exactly what he was thinking. She had told him all about the arrogant Greek who had been pursuing her. 'What the hell is going on?' he demanded.

'I . . .' Where did she start? she wondered wretchedly. And worse, where did she finish? Her tongue did a nervous flick around her dry lips, and for the life of her, she couldn't look Jason directly in the face. 'I h-had to see Mr Lakitos about something important,' she mumbled in the end.

'And it took you all night?'

She nodded, lifting her hand to her brow. Her head was thumping, the cold morning air was making her shiver, her feet were numb, and she felt utterly used up inside. 'I had to wait until Mr Lakitos was free to——'

'You spent the night with him?'

'No!' she denied, feeling her cheeks go hot, and silently cursing them for it.

'Do you think this is the kind of discussion we should be having on the doorstep of a sick man's home?' Anton Lakitos put in grimly.

'My father!' Nina gasped, horrified that she had forgotten all about him.

With a tug, she released herself from Anton Lakitos's grip, and blindly pushed by Jason to dash into the house. Sadie was standing by the bottom of the stairs, her old face drawn in deep lines of concern, and, swallowing on a bank of fear, she ran quickly up the stairs.

She couldn't go inside. Every single instinct she possessed was rebelling against the idea of entering her father's bedroom, she was so terribly afraid of what she might find.

'Easy does it,' a quiet voice murmured just behind her. She was trembling so badly that her teeth were chattering in her head, the slender body beneath the limp blouse and skirt shaking violently.

'Is he . . . ?' She couldn't ask it, the words clogging in her fear-thickened throat.

'No,' Anton Lakitos gently assured her, catching her to him when she sagged in relief. 'Apparently, he's had another attack—a minor one,' he added quickly when she turned to bury her face in his shirt, too needful of his presence to thrust him away as she should be doing. 'The doctor is with him now, and he is comfortable.'

'Thank God,' she breathed. 'I would never have forgiven myself if he'd . . .' Swallowing again, she straightened up. 'W-where is Jason?' Her gaze flicked searchingly along the softly lit landing.

'He seemed—reluctant to come near your father's room,' he remarked drily.

'Of course,' she accepted. Her father would have another attack just suspecting Jason was in the house!

God, she thought heavily, what a mess it all was. If only her father didn't resent Jason so much, he could have been a great source of comfort to him while he lay so ill. As a qualified accountant, Jason could have lifted the burden of Lovell's right from her father's shoulders—had offered to—despite the older man's aversion to him. But she hadn't even dared put the suggestion forward. It was sad that the two most important people in her life should be at such loggerheads.

'Now, if you feel ready, we will go and see your father together, and see if we cannot find a way to give him peace of mind,' Anton Lakitos said firmly. 'That is what you want, is it not?' he added when she glanced uncertainly at him.

'I—yes,' she frowned, not sure of anything any more. Perhaps, if her father could have accepted Jason, she wouldn't be standing here having to accept the help of his enemy.

'Good.' The tone was quietly satisfied. 'So pull yourself together. Pray to God your father is too exhausted to notice your atrocious state, and let us go in.'

Atrocious, he called her. Nina looked down at her cold, dirty feet, and placed a hand to the limp, wet tangle of her hair. Atrocious just about said it.

Dr Martin was just packing his bag away when they entered the room. He glanced up expectantly, showing relief when he saw her. 'Ah, Nina,' he said. 'Thank goodness. Your father has been fretting for you.'

She nodded, eyes going worriedly to the frail figure lying so still on the bed. 'H-how is he?'

'There's no fool like an old fool, so the saying goes,' he drily observed. Dr Martin was an old friend of her father's, their family practitioner for as far back as Nina could remember. 'I've got him taped this time, though.' A rueful glance at his patient said it hadn't been easy. 'He won't be trying any more silly tricks for a while.'

'What did he do?' She moved towards the bed. There was a single low-watt bulb burning beside it, illuminating the awful grey cast of her father's face.

'Got out of bed,' Dr Martin announced. 'Actually got himself as far as the phone in his study before he collapsed. Getting someone to sort some other poor bloke out, so he said—couldn't catch who, the name was too foreign for my English ears.'

'Me, probably.' Anton stepped over to offer his hand to the doctor. 'Anton Lakitos,' he introduced himself, his gaze sliding over to where Nina was now kneeling by the bed, her father's limp hand held between both of hers. 'Is he going to be all right?'

The doctor shrugged non-committally. 'I've been warning him for months to slow down. He brought these attacks on himself. Wouldn't listen to the experts, wouldn't do anything he was told to do. But then, old Jonas isn't known for his listening powers,' he concluded drily.

Anton Lakitos nodded grimly, as though in complete agreement, his gaze still fixed on Nina where she knelt talking softly to her father. Jonas Lovell's eyes were

closed, and there was no sign that he was aware she was
even there.

'I wanted to shift him to hospital when the big one
hit last week, but he wouldn't hear of it,' the doctor was
saying. 'Said if he was going to die, then he would do
it in his own bed—stubborn old mule damned near
achieved it with this last escapade. If Nina had been here,
he wouldn't have got beyond putting a foot out of the
bed, but then, she's taken enough these last few days.
He's a bloody awful patient, and I'm worried about her
too.'

'There is no need to be,' Anton Lakitos murmured,
eyes still locked on Nina's washed-out profile. 'I will be
here to share the burden with her now.'

'Nina...?' The rusty croak brought everyone's
attention to the man in the bed.

'I'm here, Daddy,' she thickly assured him.

'Where've you been?' Eyes which had once been the
same vibrant blue as his daughter's looked grey and dim
as they opened slowly to look at her. Tears split Nina's
vision, an anguished sob trapping inside her throat.

'With me, Jonas,' Anton Lakitos inserted levelly. He
had moved to stand behind Nina the moment the sick
man spoke, leaving the doctor to see himself out of the
room.

'My God,' Jonas huffed. 'You're quick off the damned
mark.' He sounded relieved rather than angry, which
completely confused his listening daughter.

'True.' A faint smile touched the younger man's face.
'But not by either your or my own persuasion, Jonas.
Your daughter came to me to plead on your behalf.'

'She did?' Surprise showed on the sick man's face.
'She's a good girl,' he whispered weakly.

'And you are a foolish old man.' Anton scolded with
an odd kind of gentleness that made Nina glance at him
in surprise. 'Things had no need to get this bad.'

'I am about to lose everything,' was the tired reply.

'You should have trusted me sooner, Jonas. Now things have gone too far, and you will have to let me deal with it all in my own way.'

'I had to try it my way first. It was my duty to try.'

'And I admire your dedication to the task,' Anton acknowledged, while Nina became more bewildered as the conversation progressed. 'But at the cost of your own health?'

'At the cost of anything!' Jonas gasped out fiercely.

'Even at the cost of your company, old man?'

It was an unfair dig, and Nina's head spun around to glare at the man standing behind her, but her father spoke first, seeming to understand and accept where she was just horribly confused.

'Yes . . .' he hissed out wearily. 'Even at the cost of that.' His weary old eyes drifted downwards, the desire to give in to the drug-induced sleep beginning to win against his resolve to stay awake. 'But it's up to you now,' Jonas conceded. 'Do your worst if you must.' The resentment towards Anton Lakitos seemed to have left him completely. 'I suppose you'll want everything now.'

'I want only one thing, and you know it.' The hand coming warm on Nina's shoulder seemed to be trying to offer comfort, but she gave an impatient shrug, annoyed at them both for talking about Lovell's as though it were a living breathing person! The hand tightened, fingers curving delicately into the rounded bone, and the sudden hectic leap of her senses brought the colour rushing to her cheeks, and she subsided, cowed by the man who seemed to be in control of all their lives now.

'Now what?' Jonas wanted to know, struggling desperately against the drugs Dr Martin had given him.

'Rest,' Anton advised. 'Leave everything to me. Then, when you are feeling stronger, we will talk.'

'About my company?' the old man asked hopefully.

'About a whole lot of things,' Anton threatened. 'Not least about the trouble you've put me to tonight. Your

daughter seems to think me a black-hearted devil, Jonas,'
he added drily.

'She does...?' A slow smile stretched the bloodless
contours of his mouth, and a hint of the old wicked
humour eased some of the strain from his face. 'She
must be confusing you with someone else,' he said, then
actually laughed as if something really funny had been
said. 'That's my girl, Nina.' Weakly, he patted her hand
where it lay beneath his own. 'Trust no man. They're
all black-hearted, man and boy alike.'

'Thanks for that vote of confidence,' Anton drawled
sardonically.

'Think nothing of it,' Jonas said, still smiling that
strange smile as he fell into instant sleep with a single
blink of a twinkling eye.

'I wish I understood a single word of all that,' Nina
sighed as she came slowly to her feet.

A hand beneath her elbow helped her rise. 'In several
ways, so do I.'

Nina glanced at him, frowning at the mockingly cryptic
reply, then shook her head. 'Whatever,' she dismissed
it all for now, too tired to struggle with it. 'Thank you
for this.' She looked back at her father, resting peace-
fully for the first time since he took ill.

Then reaction set in, sending her into a paroxysm of
shivers that had him drawing her into his arms as he
murmured roughly, 'Don't thank me yet, Nina Lovell.
You have no idea what my terms for helping you are
going to be.'

With that, he led her out of the room, his closeness
disturbing her senses all over again. 'Th-that sounded
very much like a threat to me,' she whispered shakily as
the bedroom door closed quietly behind them.

Anton Lakitos turned her in his arms, forcing her with
the superior power of his will to look at him. His eyes
were dark and hooded, but glowing with that terrible
look she had always seen written there. 'It was much
more than a threat, my beautiful nymph,' he murmured

huskily, his arms folding her hard against him. 'It was a vow...'

He kissed her then, taking her lips with a hunger that was too easily matched by her own. His mouth was warm and knowing, moving so sensually over her own that he urged a response from her without having to try very hard. And they clung together, relighting flames which had never really been doused since the incident on his bed, hours ago.

It was as his tongue tangled with hers that the horror of what she was allowing had her groaning and she dragged her mouth away from his. 'No!' she whimpered. 'Please, I can't take any more!'

'No,' he sighed. 'I don't suppose you can.' Black eyes glinted hotly down at her, and Nina trembled as she fought not to meld her mouth on to his again. 'But this isn't going to be the end of it, Nina Lovell,' he warned raspingly. 'And the quicker you come to terms with that, the better it will be for all of us!'

They stared at each other for a moment, the awful truth in what he was saying holding her trapped in sheer horror of it. Then he growled, the sound coming from deep inside his cavernous chest, and his mouth caught hers again with a swift but lethal kiss which left her emotions naked.

'Which is your room?' His gaze flicked impatiently along the landing.

Nina just pointed, too weak to do much more. But when he bent to swing her into his arms she came alive in a way that sent the dizziness flying. 'No, Anton!' she cried out hoarsely. 'You can't——!'

'I can,' he growled. 'And if I wished to I would!' The door opened inwards with a jerk, and he swung them both inside. 'But now is not the time, nor the place for what you have in mind, and I am, though you probably don't believe it, not so insensitive as to make love to you here, with your father lying ill not far away, and your fiancé waiting downstairs!'

Jason! she thought with a shiver of guilt. Once again, she had forgotten all about Jason!

He dropped her feet to the floor, keeping hold of her only long enough to be sure she was steady before he let go and moved right away from her, taking only a small amount of the violent static emanating between them with him. 'Now,' he went on grimly, 'you will shower yourself into some semblance of sanity, and change your bedraggled clothes, then we will talk, you and I. Talk,' he repeated for a second ominous-sounding time. 'Before we go and deal with that angry fiancé of yours!'

'We?' She was still trembling from that kiss he had just branded her with, literally pulsing with a need to throw herself at him. Appalled at herself, at him, at everything, she turned angrily on him. 'What do you mean—we? There is no we about it! Any explanations which need to be made to Jason will be done in private!'

'How long have you been involved with him?'

'What has that got to do with you?' she cried.

His eyes grew hard. 'Don't, Nina, make the mistake of trying to challenge me,' he grimly warned. 'How long?'

'F-five, maybe six months,' she answered in a subdued voice, niggled at how easily she backed down.

The grimness increased. 'And your father, how has he responded to the association?'

She shifted uncomfortably where she stood. 'I...he—he's prejudiced against Jason,' she reluctantly admitted. 'My father and Jason's were partners years ago. They had a row, and he's never forgotten it.'

'But you just never bothered trying to find out why?'

Yes, she had tried. But it had been a hard, black period in her father's life, and she had been very young, and she didn't blame her father for not wanting to remember it. In a few short months he had lost his wife in a terrible car accident, and then his best friend and business partner through a row that had been so bitter that it had persisted through all the years that followed it.

Grief-stricken and disillusioned, he had buried himself in his work, cutting everything else out—herself out to a certain extent. Lovell's had become his great passion. Then along had come this man, determined to take even that away from him!

'Hell,' Anton muttered suddenly. 'It's no wonder Jonas is going out of his mind!'

'And whose fault is that?' she cried, stung by his condemning tone. 'You've been lying and cheating your way into my father's life since the first day you met him. It's down to you that he's lying where he is now, worrying himself to death about some awful deal you're obviously forcing on him, and no one, not even my father, can blame Jason for that!'

His gaze slewed back to clash with hers, and something dark and nasty passed between them, something which had Nina physically backing away though he didn't move a single muscle towards her.

'Go and get that shower,' he advised, 'before I change my mind about my own sensitivity and throw you on to that bed to make love to you until you can't remember your own name, never mind that of your damned fiancé!'

She went; a single second longer holding on to that suddenly threatening gaze had her stumbling across the room to lock herself behind the relative sanctuary of her connecting bathroom door.

When she came back, he was relaxing in her window seat. It was fully light outside now, though the overcast sky could do little to lift the heavy mood from the pretty blue and peach room.

'I need to fetch some clean clothes,' she mumbled, defiantly aware of the inadequacy of the short towelling robe she was wearing.

Her hair lay in a thick wet pelt down her back, the warmth of the shower had put some colour back into her cheeks, and she was angry, angry at the lingering sensations she was having to deal with because of this man, angry at the way he had so casually staked claim over her life.

Anton lifted his head, eyes hooding lazily as they ran over her, taking in everything from the warm moist V of creamy skin at her throat to the long length of slender leg left exposed by the skimpy cut of the robe. By the time he lifted his black eyes to hers, she was blushing fiercely, and hating both of them for it.

A nerve twitched a bit of wry humour into the edges of his mouth. 'Perhaps I should call your fiancé in here right now...' he mused cruelly. 'Then there would be no need for explanations of any kind.'

'God, you're despicable,' she breathed, moving stiffly across the room to throw open her wardrobe doors. 'You think you can take control of people the way you can your petty companies. Well...' she turned to glare at him '...I am not for sale, Mr Lakitos. Just remember that when Jason is around, because if it were a choice between you and him I would choose Jason any day!

'So, you are not for sale, heh?' He didn't sound angry, just curious.

Nina sent him a disdainful look before she turned her attention back to the contents of her wardrobe. 'No,' she said, and snatched a pair of cream linen trousers from their hanger. 'I love Jason!' she announced forcefully. And she did, she told herself desperately. She did! 'And, as soon as my father is well enough to hear the news, I will be marrying him!'

'You will not,' Anton Lakitos smoothly drawled, 'because, Miss Lovell, you will be marrying me.'

Nina went still, the pale green silk shirt she had been about to pull from its hanger sliding uselessly through her fingers as she stood, trying to convince herself that she had misheard that last incredible statement.

'What did you say?' she demanded breathlessly, once she could get her throat muscles to unlock.

'You heard,' he said, eyeing her coolly. 'You've known how badly I want you from the moment I set eyes on you, so why are you looking so shocked?'

Because want and marriage were two completely separate issues. Something clamoured inside her, then settled to a quiver low down in her stomach. She reached up and pulled the shirt from its hanger. Trying to appear calm, she laid the clean clothes on the bed, then moved to the tall chest of drawers to slide open the top drawer. 'And you heard me,' she said as carelessly as she could in the circumstances. 'Thank you, but no, thank you. Jason is the man I love, and he is the man I will marry.'

'Sit down, Nina, you're trembling,' was all he said, and she turned on him like a virago.

'Will you just get out of here and leave me alone?'

'No.' The dark head shook, black eyes intent on her.

'What is it you want from me?' she cried, suddenly so agitated she didn't even know she was clutching a pair of fine white lacy briefs in her hands, tugging and stretching at the delicate fabric in a way which brought a rueful twist to her tormentor's attractive mouth. 'An apology?' she asked shrilly. 'Is that it? You want an apology for the way I broke into your house and hit out at you and insulted you?'

'Don't forget the way you tried to seduce me,' he reminded her lazily.

'I did not try to seduce you!' Almost stamping a childish foot in frustration, Nina saw the humour in his gaze too late to realise how beautifully she had risen to his bait. 'Stop being so flippant,' she muttered, at last seeing the mangled briefs and stuffing them quickly back in the drawer, her cheeks on fire.

'Then stop trying to convince me that you love that young fool downstairs,' Anton threw derisively back. 'My God,' he sighed, all hint of humour leaving him as he got up while she stood dry-mouthed watching the lithe movement of his long body. 'He can't be more than a year older than you.'

'Three,' she corrected.

'He looks younger,' he growled, shoving his hands into his trouser pockets.

'And how old are you?' Nina decided to get in a few taunts of her own. 'Thirty-one—thirty-two?'

'Thirty-four actually.' His grimace acknowledged the fourteen-year gap between himself and Nina.

But she rubbed it in anyway. 'And you think that makes you more acceptable to me than Jason? I don't know whether that makes you a cradle-snatcher, or just an ageing old——'

'Watch it,' he warned, and her tongue cleaved itself to the roof of her mouth, as she became aware that once again she had almost gone too far with this frighteningly aggravating man. 'I'll tell you this much, Nina Lovell,' he went on grimly. 'I may seem old to you, but just try turning those kisses you branded on me on to your precious Jason and see what he does! He's not man enough for a hot-natured little siren like you. Marry him, and you'll burn him out in a night—or, worse, hide your own desires behind a scenario of invented gasps and contrived shudders while you burn with frustration inside rather than frighten your poor darling Jason!'

'God, you're so crude!' she choked, turning her back on him so she could hide the look of mortified truth written on her face. She had never allowed Jason to kiss her like this man had. Nor had she ever felt the desire to kiss Jason as she had kissed Anton Lakitos!

'It is crude,' he derided, 'to sentence you both to that kind of pathetic relationship. You think you will be happy with it? Do you think he will be?'

He won't know, Nina thought, then shocked herself rigid with what she was actually admitting to herself. 'Oh, hell,' she groaned, slumping her slender shoulders. 'I hate you.'

'Well, that is a whole lot healthier an emotion than the kind of brotherly love you feel for him,' he snapped irritably. 'And I will promise you this much, Nina

Lovell——' He reached out to take her by the shoulders, bringing her to stand in front of him, the fire and the passion alight in his eyes as he glared dwon at her, put there by the anger throbbing between them '—marry me, and I'll match those wonderful passions of yours, fire by fire, ache by ecstatic ache!'

'Stop it!' she whispered, beginning to tremble. Her hand snaked up to clutch at the gaping folds of her robe, her heart accelerating out of control as she stared darkly up at him. She was falling into the fathomless blackness of his eyes again, drawn by the fire, the need to feel its heat, to feel his body weighing heavily on her own again!

'You'll marry me,' he pushed on relentlessly, the words rasping from his throat, grating along her every sense, tripping live wires of feeling as they went. 'For your own sake! But if you can't bring yourself to accept the truth in that then you will marry me for your father's sake, because it is the only way he will keep his company!'

'No!' she breathed, trying to pull away from him.

'Yes,' he hissed, long fingers winding around the thick wet pelt of hair so he could tilt her head back until the creamy length of her throat was exposed to his passionate gaze. 'Feel this?' he murmured huskily, placing the moist tip of his tongue against the pulse-point pounding in her throat so that it leapt, throbbing all the faster. 'That is what I can do to you with just a simple caress! Marry me, Nina,' he urged, 'and I will promise you that neither you nor your father will suffer by my hand.' He buried his face in her throat, the taunting tongue trailing fire as it slid across her sensitive skin.

His body throbbed against her own, hard-packed and shockingly aroused. Nina gasped, struggling to fight against the thick clouds of sensual need he was wrapping around her. 'Please . . . !' she whimpered. 'Don't do this to me!'

'Marry me,' he pushed on passionately, 'And I will even forgo all the money your father owes me, every last——'

'He owes you money?' If anything had the power to tumble her back to hard reality, then that piece of information did.

'You didn't know?' Anton let loose a soft curse, sounding angry with himself. He allowed her to put a few desperately needed inches between them. 'Of course he owes me money,' he muttered. 'He owes me a damn sight more than his company is worth,' he informed her grimly. 'More than you could even begin to appreciate.'

'Oh, God.' She sagged all over again, this new shock sending her reeling into a whole new nightmare.

Strong hands moulded the rounded bones in her shoulders. 'He borrowed a large amount of money from me several months ago to pay off some—large debts he had acquired, and put up Lovell's as security against the loan. He was supposed to pay me back within three months, but he hadn't a cat in hell's chance of doing that while——'

'Then why did you lend it him, if you knew he couldn't pay you back?'

He didn't answer, his hard mouth snapping shut as if he'd said too much already.

Nina's eyes narrowed on his closed face. 'Unless you did it for that reason,' she therefore concluded, pulling right away from him. 'Because you knew he couldn't pay you back, and the company would be yours anyway.'

His hands dropped wearily to his sides. 'I thought I had just explained to you that he owes me more than Lovell's is worth.'

'Then what other reason could you have had to throw good money after bad?'

'You already know the answer to that, Nina.' His eyes held hers for a long and killing moment before he added huskily, 'You.'

'Don't...' Icy shivers went slinking down her spine, and she turned her back on him, arms going up to wrap tightly around herself. 'You're frightening me.'

'I frighten myself, believe me. I have never in my entire life wanted a woman as badly as I want you!' He came to stand right behind her, his fingers running in un-hidden agitation along her towelling-covered arms. 'And if you think I like it any more than you do, then think again! But at least admit it is the same for you,' he ground out huskily. 'Even if you cannot say it out loud to me!'

He turned her then, catching the horror of truth in her eyes and growling at it just before his mouth hit hers with enough force to knock any attempt at denial right back down her throat.

His hard body pressed against the fragile softness of her own. Hot, dark and excitingly alien. He burned for her, and it was knowing that which lit an answering fire inside herself. Her arms went up, sliding along the soft wool knit of his jumper, fingers spreading out to trace the ripple of muscle beneath, muscles she had been yearning to touch again ever since her hands had made contact with them in the pitch-black battle on his bed.

He shuddered, groaning against her straining mouth, and she shuddered too, her spine arching upwards as his hand slipped inside her robe to search out her waiting breasts. His fingers trembled as they caressed her, and she bloomed for him, aware only of the man and the kiss and what his touch was doing to her.

The kiss deepened, and the robe slid smoothly from her shoulders, his arms trapping her to him as he made her feel the force of his desire for her. There was some-thing incredibly erotic in having her naked breasts crushed against the rough texture of pure wool. She felt frail and helpless in his arms, so very feminine, that she moved enticingly against him.

The knock at the door was a mere hearsay before it flew open, the solid wood banging back against the opposite wall, allowing Jason to walk angrily in on them.

CHAPTER FOUR

'Do YOU usually barge into someone's bedroom without invitation?' Anton gained his composure a whole lot quicker than Nina could, speaking calmly into the drumming silence while she just stood there shaking, feeling Jason's pained abhorrence as if it were her own.

'How long has this been going on?' he bit out harshly.

'Long enough,' Anton replied, smoothly shifting his body until he was effectively hiding Nina from view by the superior height and width of him. Then, with a slow deliberation, he began straightening her robe, sliding it back over her shoulders and tucking it gently beneath her lowered chin, her mortification obvious by the dark red flush colouring her cheeks. She felt his mouth move lightly over the top of her head, and trembled on a remnant of desire, her fingers clutching at him for support. His hand came to lift her chin, black eyes searching her pained and guilty face, going grim at the sight of shamed tears glinting in her blue eyes. 'Ssh,' he murmured, and kissed her softly on her trembling mouth.

'God, will you leave her alone?' Jason grated in thickened disgust. 'She's wearing my ring, for God's sake!'

'An opportune move on your part, I think,' Anton said quietly.

'What's that supposed to mean?' Jason demanded.

'Oh, I think you know.' Anton twisted his dark head to level Jason with a look. 'It would be advisable to close the door if you don't wish to be overheard.'

The door slammed shut, and Nina winced, struggling to pull herself together, placing the palms of her hands against the rock-hard wall of the chest she was trapped against, and Anton let her go, watching grimly as she drew herself up and took a deep breath before stepping around him to face her fiancé.

Tall and reed-slender, he looked demolished, and her heart wept. His face was as pale as his light blond hair, grey eyes silver with shock. He was staring at Anton Lakitos as though he'd just thrust a knife into his chest.

The silver eyes slid sideways to accuse her. 'You're lovers, aren't you?'

Nina swallowed, tears backing up in her tight throat. 'I...'

'Yes, we are lovers,' the man beside her answered for her.

'I wasn't speaking to you!' Jason sliced at him, eyes flashing a hatred Nina could well understand. 'Nina...?' he appealed hoarsely.

She stared mutely at him. What could she say? Her heart was bleeding for him, for herself and the terrible mess she had placed them all in with her madness tonight. But the awful truth of it was, she and Anton had become lovers tonight. Oh, maybe not in the way Jason was thinking, but as near as mattered. She lowered her head, and said nothing.

'I should have guessed!' he rasped, shock turning to bitter contempt. 'When you first mentioned the damned Greek's name to me, I should have guessed your father was up to something!—I should have remembered how history has a habit of repeating itself! You Lovells have always meant the kiss of death to my family!'

'Oh, no, please, Jason!' Nina pleaded painfully. 'You have it all wrong, my father didn't have anything to do with——'

'Of course it's his doing!' he derided, eyes lashing her with scorn. 'He hates me enough to do anything to stop you marrying me! The conniving devil has set you up— and you're so damned stupid, you don't even know it!'

He had good excuse to feel maligned by the Lovells, Nina acknowledged as a fresh wave of guilt washed over her. History was repeating itself in a way. Ten years ago, when their two fathers had had their blistering row, Jason's father had been the one to lose out to the much shrewder Jonas who had quite ruthlessly forced Michael Hunter out of Lovell Hunter, even going as far as to have the Hunter name taken from the company. Michael Hunter had never succeeded in business again after that. According to Jason, he had died a year ago a bitterly disillusioned man.

'I'm sorry that my father refuses to accept you, Jason,' she whispered huskily, ashamed as always at the way her father had stubbornly refused to let the past die. Even though Jason had been quite prepared to let it go—for her sake, she acknowledged painfully. He had been prepared to put his own resentments aside for her sake.

She lifted pained and guilty eyes to his. 'But this has nothing to do with my father,' she insisted. 'This,' she sighed, 'is all my fault.'

'You're damned right it's all your fault!' He was literally throbbing with anger and wounded pride, the hard look in his eyes withering her where she stood. 'If you hadn't been such a gullible fool, we could have had everything. Everything!'

'And now you will leave here with nothing,' a grim voice put in, its total lack of compassion so cruel that Nina gasped at it.

'For goodness' sake!' She turned on him, a trembling hand going up to touch her brow in despair. 'Why are you doing this?'

'Yes, Mr Lakitos...' Jason sneeringly provoked. 'Why are you doing it?'

It was a challenge, and one so deadly serious that the whole room seemed to go still. Anton stood to one side of her, his poise so finely balanced that Nina could feel the tension emanating from him, and held her breath, sensing that something utterly destructive was being tempted out into the open, although what it was she had no idea, only that the threat was definitely there.

Then Anton moved, his hands coming warm and possessive around her waist, ruthlessly staking claim. 'Nina came to me,' he stated the unpalatable truth of it, 'and to me she has given herself. Unlike old Jonas, I share nothing—nothing. Do you understand?'

'And you expect me to just accept that and walk meekly away?' A finely etched eyebrow rose in calculated challenge. The anger seemed to have gone from Jason, leaving a hard, cold shell behind it, and she found herself staring at a stranger. A tall, fair, bitterly cynical stranger. And it was as if she weren't the issue here any longer, dismissed by something far more important. 'She's wearing my ring, remember?' he added smoothly. 'Surely that must count for something?'

'Ah, yes,' Anton drawled, 'The ring.' One of his hands left her waist to grasp her left hand, lifting it out in front of them, then slowly, carefully, while the tears washed her eyes all over again, he slid the small solitaire from her finger, twisting it thoughtfully between finger and thumb. 'And what price do you put on your—broken heart, Hunter?' he enquired curiously, and, while Nina choked in horror at his filthy suggestion, he named a figure that had her going rigid with shock.

'Double that may be nearer the mark.'

'Oh, Jason,' she choked, feeling the nausea begin churning inside.

'Done,' Anton said, and threw the ring to Jason, who caught it deftly. The smile he turned on Nina was hard and contemptuous. 'What does it feel like to be sold down the river for the price of a Rolls-Royce?' he taunted her.

She shuddered, the sickness almost overwhelming her. He had done it to get his revenge on her, accepted Anton's offer because he'd known it would hurt her more than anything else he could have said or done.

'Here...' She looked up in time to see the diamond ring floating through the air towards her, and caught it instinctively. 'Keep it as a memento,' he invited as he opened the door. 'I certainly don't want it—any more than I want you.' He turned to slice them both with an insolent glance. 'Second-hand goods were never to my taste. Don't forget the money, Lakitos. I am not by nature a very patient man.'

Then he was gone, striding out of the room and out of Nina's life, leaving the atmosphere thick and tainted behind him.

Nina sank down heavily on the edge of the bed. 'I'll never forgive you for this,' she whispered thickly. She knew Jason, and all that careless insolence had just been a front he'd erected to hide his real pain behind. It was the same careless insolence he had used to hide her father's hostile rejection of him. The same careless insolence he had shown when he told her about the straitened circumstances of his upbringing after his father and hers broke apart. And now he had used it to hide his feelings of hurt and betrayal. 'Isn't it enough that you want to ruin my father—did you have to ruin my happiness too?'

Anton spun his back to her. 'I don't remember promising you happiness, Nina,' he murmured flatly.

'I wasn't talking about any hope of happiness with you!' she cried scathingly.

'You honestly believe you would have been happy with that mercenary devil?' If she had thought her own tone scornful, then his eclipsed it.

'He needed to leave with his pride,' she explained, staring at the small diamond lying in the palm of her hand. Betrayer, it seemed to be accusing her. Betrayer—and she shuddered. 'The only way he could do that was by making me appear insignificant next to your blood money. You men and your damned pride,' she sighed, thinking of her father who had been prepared to die for his precious pride. 'You live and die by it, but what about my pride, my self-respect?' she demanded thickly. 'I don't think I shall ever feel clean again!'

'And you blame me for this also? You came to me for help, Nina,' he reminded her. 'Not the other way around.'

'I should have gone straight to Jason,' she whispered, still gazing tearfully at the ring.

'Perhaps you should,' he agreed, sounding infinitely weary of the whole affair, 'but you didn't. And now you must pay the price for your mistake!'

Without her expecting it, he reached down and pulled her to her feet. His eyes glinted black fire at her as he wrenched the ring from her and slid it arrogantly into his pocket.

'Forget Hunter and his damned ring,' he bit out roughly. 'You belong to me now!' Before she could do more than gasp out a protest, she was in his arms, and the kiss was hard and punishing, but staking claim all over again. By the time he let go of her, she was trembling badly, and the tears of sensual defeat were hot in her eyes.

'An—interesting price, is it not, *agapi mou*?' he taunted cruelly, sounding more huskily Greek than he had ever done. His gaze narrowed meaningfully on the parted fullness of her kiss-swollen lips. 'One, I think, you are more than willing to pay.'

He put her from him, contempt at her easy submission twisting his hard features as he moved right away from her, and Nina sank back on to the bed, head lowering in weary defeat.

'I want your solemn promise that you will tell me if Hunter tries to make contact with you,' Anton said suddenly, bringing her head shooting right up again.

'But why?' she asked bewilderedly. 'He isn't likely to do that. Not after what I've just done to him! He would cut me dead rather than speak to me again.'

His eyes hooded over. 'Nevertheless,' he insisted, 'I want that promise.'

Nina stared at his grim face for a moment, then shrugged. 'All right,' she said. 'You have it—for what good it will do you. But I won't be hearing from Jason again.'

'I hope sincerely that you are right,' he murmured grimly. 'I *prefer* to hope you are right, for your sake, Nina, as well as his...'

The first letter arrived only three days later, proving her wrong and Anton Lakitos right. Jason wrote with all the pain and passion he was feeling right now, and his words confirmed her belief in him.

> I ripped up the cheque from Lakitos. I only accepted his bribe because I knew it would hurt you, but all the money in the world couldn't make up for the loss I'm suffering now. I loved you— still love you, and, no matter how the evidence of my own eyes wants to tell me otherwise, I can't believe you would willingly wish to hurt me like this. It has to be an elaborate scheme to break us up. Your father has always hated me, enough to make sure I never become a member of your family. Can you bring yourself to meet with me, darling? So we can talk? Call me, I need to see you. I need to understand...

With tears of misery in her eyes, Nina sat in her father's study with the letter clutched in her hands, desperately torn between a desire to do as Jason begged, and go and see him, at least try to explain, and the heavy knowledge that explanations would not change anything.

She was trapped, and she knew it. Trapped by her own reckless stupidity and concern for her father. And she forced herself to admit the full and chilling truth about her own weak character. From the moment Anton Lakitos had kissed her, her feelings for Jason had faded into the shadows of her life.

Getting up, she stood over the waste-paper basket, and let the letter fall into it, tears blinding her eyes as it slithered hollowly to the bottom. Discarded, she made the comparison as she walked away; discarded, just like Jason.

It was a week before Jonas Lovell was deemed fit enough for that talk that had been promised by Anton. And it was a week when Nina learned the full torment of her own wretched anxieties, aided and abetted by the steady flow of correspondence she received daily from Jason. In one letter he posed a telling question.

> Have you asked yourself why Lakitos is so willing to help in the conspiracy against us? Lovell's owns some very lucrative property in the centre of London. Property which any speculator would give his eye teeth to obtain. Ask your father if you don't believe me. Lovell's is suffering from a worrying cash-flow problem at the moment, but nothing that could not be put right once your father is well again. But who aims to gain if the worst should happen and your father does not recover? I am concerned, Nina, dreadfully concerned that Lakitos is manipulating you into his clutches to get his hands on Lovell's. We have to meet again, if only to discuss my suspicions...

Could Anton have lied when he had said Lovell's was worth less than her father already owed him?

The letter went the same way as all the others, while her emotions flittered through a whole new set of uncertainties. And, as if to confirm all Jason's suspicions, Anton himself had become so cool and remote that she shivered when he came into the room. A man who professed an uncontrollable desire for her, he had barely glanced at her since declaring it!

He called around every day, asked about her father, asked about herself with all the polite interest of a stranger, then retired to her father's study to go diligently through the sick man's mail before he left again, leaving her wondering if the madness they had shared had already burned itself out!

By the time a week was over, every single resentful feeling she'd ever felt towards Anton Lakitos had re-asserted itself, and the only softening of this frame of mind that she would allow herself was a small gratitude for the change he had helped bring about in her father. Jonas was working hard at getting well now instead of waiting to die. The spark of life was back in his eyes, and, where before he had been restless and awkward to deal with, now he was content to rest and willing to please, which, in that contrary way things had of playing with your feelings, Nina resented because he had not wanted to get better for her sake, but the mere glimmer of hope where his company was concerned had worked wonders!

'The doctor thinks it will be OK for me to speak to your father today,' Anton coolly informed her when he arrived one morning, looking so much the powerful businessman in his dark, sophisticated suit and snowy white linen shirt that Nina went dry-mouthed just looking at him.

'Change your mind,' she pleaded impulsively.

They were standing in the hall, he towering over her and looking every one of his daunting thirty-four years with that austere expression he was wearing on his face, and she feeling so painfully young and ill-equipped to deal with this man who had so thoroughly taken over her life.

'In what way exactly?' he drawled unapproachably.

His cool gaze was fixed on her face, and each individual pore was tingling as if he'd reached out and caressed her. She shivered delicately, her slender hands clutching together across the simple pale lemon cotton knit dress she was wearing.

'A-about marrying me,' she stammered. 'I—you—we don't even like each other!' she cried out desperately, seeing no hint of softening in his hard face.

'We don't have to like each other to feel what we do for each other,' he oh, so cynically pointed out.

'It was a silly—crazy night, when everything got out of hand! Can't you just—just give my father more time to pay back the money he owes you, then leave it at that?' she suggested hopefully.

'But you forget,' he said, seeming fascinated by her agitation, 'it isn't Lovell's I want.' His narrowed gaze dared her to challenge him. 'It is you I want,' he stated silkily when she said nothing but only looked more hunted. 'And it is for you that I am going against all my better instincts and allowing him to heap all his problems on to me!'

'I'll hate you until the day I die if you make me go through with it!' she vowed hectically.

'Then hate me!' he snapped, suddenly losing all that ice-cold reserve and reaching out to pull her to him. 'But marry me you will! Or I'll take you without the respectability of the ring, and your father will get nothing—not one concession from me!'

She was trembling. The moment he touched her the heat began burning its sensual trail through her body. He glared down at her, the light of desire thoroughly lit in his eyes, eating her, consuming her in the deep dark blackness so that she cried out, a choked, husky little sound that drew an answering groan from him just before his mouth took hers in a kiss that sent her flying back across the fraught days to a night when this man had changed the whole course of her desires.

'Deny that, if you dare,' he challenged as he drew away. She was breathing heavily, hardly able to lift her drugged lids from her eyes. 'You want me, Nina,' he claimed raspingly. 'It sings as powerfully in your blood as it does in mine!'

'I'm afraid of you,' she whispered wretchedly.

'I know.' He loosened his grip on her, moving his hands along her spine to gently cup her nape beneath the fine silk fall of her hair. 'But I think you are even more afraid of yourself.'

His thumbs drew lazy caressing circles on the soft skin at her jawline, his expression brooding as he looked down at her pale, anxious face. Then he let her go, sighing softly as he did so.

'Why not make this easy on yourself, and pretend you are in love with me?' His voice was loaded with a sardonic whimsy that made her shiver. 'You never know,' he went on drily, 'if you work hard enough at it, you may even manage to convince me! There is a lot of power in a woman's love for her man, Nina. It can buy her everything she could ever desire.'

'Except the man she really loves.'

'Don't start that again.' He turned away from her, sounding wearied to death as he moved towards the stairs. 'Just remember when you see your father next to make him believe we are besotted with each other.'

'Anton?' she called out hesitantly as his foot took the first stair. He stopped, turning slowly back to face her. Nina stared at him, her lovely eyes despising him, even as they drank him up. 'I w-want to know how long this— sentence you're inflicting on me has to last.'

His eyes narrowed, and he suddenly looked very much the arrogant Greek. 'Explain,' he clipped, nothing else; the hard-hearted businessman was back on show, and he used a harsh economy of words, most of them cuttingly intimidating.

Nina swallowed tensely. 'If I agree to m-marry you——'

'You already have agreed,' he pointed out, reinforcing that remark by glancing at her kiss-swollen mouth.

She flushed, her lips quivering a little as she pushed herself to say what she had been working up to say to him all week. 'You must know that the doctors have warned me not to expect my father to...' She couldn't say it, the word just got stuck in her throat. 'The day he—goes...' she went for the closest substitute, 'is the day any commitment I make to you ends also.'

He didn't say anything for a while, and the tension in the hallway inched itself up a few more notches while those narrowed eyes continued to study her pale young face with its small determined chin and anxiously staring eyes. She was aware that she had no bargaining power here. She had given all that up the night she had begged him for his help. Anton Lakitos wanted her. And, God help her, she wanted him. She had no weapons to fight him with. She only had to look at him to have her newly awakened senses screaming.

His nod of agreement was curt and grim. 'All right,' he said at last. 'If—when the time comes, and you still wish to dissolve our marriage, then I won't stop you.'

'Thank you,' she whispered, aware that he had allowed her that one concession where none was due.

'Oh, don't thank me, Nina,' he drawled, the sardonic man well and truly back in place. 'After all,' he pointed out, 'the condition will automatically apply to me as well as to you. I may well be glad to see the back of you by then.'

Those hard black eyes held hers for a moment longer, and she felt their impact with an ice-cold shiver that struck deeply into her, washing the colour right out of her face. A slow smile stretched the hard contours of his mouth. He had won that round, just as he won every battle they waged with each other. He wanted her, and had made no secret of the fact. But it wasn't love, and sexual desire could wither and die as quickly as it had risen to life. She had only demanded of him what he himself wanted. A loophole, to free himself when this awful gnawing ache had left him.

He turned away from her and began climbing the stairs while she watched him go, numbed into silence as something terrible shuddered through her.

No! she denied its terrible warning, and spun away from the tall, lean sight of him, shivering violently at the suspicion that she was halfway to loving him already.

She hadn't been able to get him out of her mind since the first time he had levelled those hungry eyes on her. She'd held him at arm's length then, not understanding why, but certain that she didn't dare let him come close to her. Now she had to wonder if her instincts had always known he could be a real threat to her very existence.

Anton Lakitos was a man of deep-running passions. She had seen him with at least four different women on different occasions, each of them clinging seductively to his side, as familiar as only lovers could be. She had known then that she could never compete on that sophisticated level. And there had been Jason, dear, caring Jason, who posed no threat to her emotions at all.

Pain streaked through her at that final confession, the ever-present guilt withering her insides as she began to acknowledge, truly acknowledge how carelessly she had confused her friendship with Jason for love.

Jason had a right to hate and despise her. And she couldn't understand why he didn't. She hated and despised herself—and Anton Lakitos because he had forced her to recognise her own sleeping devils within.

It was an hour before she found the courage to go into her father's bedroom, her troubled thoughts putting the bruises back around her eyes.

Jonas was resting against a mountain of pillows, talking genially to Anton who was relaxing in the chair in which Nina had spent her long hours of vigil when her father had been so gravely ill.

'So.' Her father smiled when he saw her. 'You've come to your senses about Hunter at last.' He sounded relieved, which only helped to chafe at her conscience. 'You two were never meant for each other,' he huffed out pompously.

Meant for each other or not, she and Jason could have been very happy together. They shared the same likes and dislikes. Their accidental meeting had come about when Jason had joined the same music group she belonged to. It had been such a wonderful surprise then,

to find out he was the same Jason Hunter she hadn't
seen since they had both been small children. They had
got on well together from the very beginning, and even
the bitterness that had remained firm between their two
fathers throughout the years hadn't been enough to stop
them wanting to be together.

It had taken Anton Lakitos to do that, and she glared
her loathing at him across the room. What interest did
they share, except this animal desire for each other's
body?

He caught the look and fielded it with a quizzical tilt
of one dark brow, then lifted his hand in arrogant
command that she go to him. Gritting her teeth, she went
obediently, flushing with embarrassed annoyance that
he didn't just stop at taking her hand, but drew her down
on to his lap.

'Your father gives us his blessing, *matia mou*,' he
murmured warmly, his fingers snaking around her trim
waist to issue a sharp dig of warning that she put a convincing smile on her face.

The smile arrived, pinned there by sheer strength of
will. A look passed between the two men, one which had
her puzzling over its meaning. Could Jason be right? she
wondered suspiciously. Had her father been plotting for
this result the whole time? She recalled how cross he had
used to get every time she rebuffed Anton's approaches
towards her. Then she dismissed the idea as unworthy.
Even her father, for all his faults, couldn't produce a
heart attack just to make his daughter toe the line.

'You make a magnificent couple.' Jonas was smiling
appreciatively at them. 'Can't wait to see the grand-
children you'll give me! Be an interesting mixture, if my
guess is right!'

Something stirred deep inside her, what, she couldn't
explain, but Anton felt it too, because he shifted tensely
beneath her, and a shower of electric sparks brought
goose-bumps out on her skin.

'I think, if you can be patient for a while, Jonas,' Anton murmured, the warmth of his body suddenly too intimate for Nina to draw breath easily, 'we will wait for a while for the children. Nina has years ahead of her to play mother. Let her become used to being a wife first, then——'

'Rubbish!' Jonas dismissed. 'The younger the better is my motto! Why, Nina's mother was only a year or so older than Nina is now when she gave birth to her!

And she's dead, Nina thought heavily. After spending a life trying her best to please a man who made no secret that his real love was his company, and the excitement it alone gave him.

She got up, her feelings in utter turmoil yet again. Was she destined for a similar fate to her mother's? Tied to a loveless marriage with a man who offered nothing more than the physical satiation of his body? What could children do, but trap her irrevocably into that kind of hell? In the end, her mother had not been able to take her unhappiness any more, and she had left, packed her bags and left both her husband and her child. 'I'm sorry,' her note had said. That was all. Not even a word of love for Nina. She had died, ironically, not by her own hand, but by that of a drunken driver who had thought he could drive faster than the wet roads would allow.

Yet something had stirred inside her at the idea of having Anton's child. A natural maternal stirring, maybe, or something much—much more frightening.

Folding her arms across her breasts and moving right away from both men, she could feel their eyes on her, her father's in mild surprise, and Anton's with a deep burning intensity.

'As I said,' he placed quietly into the silence, 'we have plenty of time to make those kinds of decisions.'

'But, Anton, you and I were just——'

'It's time I left, Jonas,' Anton cut in brusquely, leaving the older man gaping as he got up from the chair, his eyes, hooded by thick frowning brows, fixed on Nina. 'Nina?' he summoned quietly.

She was standing across the room, staring at the portrait which hung over the fireplace, studying the beautiful smiling face of her mother, painted at a time when she had been happy with them. I will never desert a child of mine! she thought fiercely. Never!

'Nina...' The deeply compelling voice had her turning slowly to face him. His hand was held out in invitation, and she found herself staring unblinkingly at it, feeling oddly shut off from the world. The hand remained outstretched and waiting, palm up, long fingers curved invitingly at the ends, as though urging her to go to him.

As if in a dream she went, pulled by a force far stronger than her own will. When she reached him, she unclipped her fingers from where they were biting into the opposite arm. She was so tense she couldn't seem to breathe properly, a dark sense of her own entity holding her in a strange void somewhere between the now and the never.

His fingers closed around her own and she watched them curl, drawn, fascinated by them, by their warmth, and the pulse of life they seemed to be transferring to her. She sucked in a deep breath then let it out again shakily, and Anton's frown darkened into concern.

With only a muttered farewell to her father, he drew her out of the room and along the landing, his grip firm but gentle as he took her down the stairs and out of the front door.

The sunlight blinded for a moment and she winced. His car stood by the front steps, its long sleek lines unnervingly familiar to her. He saw her inside then moved around to get in beside her, driving away without a single enquiry as to whether she wanted to go with him or not.

CHAPTER FIVE

'WHEN was the last time you stepped out of that house?' Anton turned to glance frowningly at Nina then away again, long hands resting lightly on the steering-wheel.

'I can't remember,' she answered vaguely, looking out of the side window at the blur of passing scenery. She still felt strange, so utterly depressed that she could barely summon up the energy to speak.

'Have you been out since I took you home last week?'

She thought about it, then shook her head. No, she hadn't been out. She had been too busy grappling with the conundrum her life had become to do anything else but brood. Not least through the fault of Jason's letters. She had written him a long letter in an attempt to explain, but had never posted it. It hadn't seemed to do anything but offer him encouragement to hope when none was there. Whatever strange paths her life took from now on, they would not be leading her back to Jason. The man sitting beside her had seen to that, with the ruthless power of his sensuality and the control he held over her father's destiny. Jason was now a part of her past, and a guilty part too. She didn't think she would ever learn to forgive herself for the way she had hurt him.

'Where are you taking me?' she enquired listlessly.

'Somewhere where you can unwind a little.' She received another searching glance from those frowning black eyes. 'You are very near a complete mental collapse, you do know that, don't you?'

Am I? she wondered. Then, yes, perhaps I am. Again, the fault of the man sitting beside her. It was the stress of confusion that did it. She just couldn't understand how, in the space of a few short hours, Anton Lakitos could have gone from being her father's sworn enemy to his most trusted friend! But every time she'd tried to broach the subject her father had shied right away from answering it, mumbling something about better the devil you know than the one you don't, and then become so anxious that she had had to drop the subject. None of it seemed to add up, least of all, why, knowing all she did know, she still only had to glance at the man sitting beside her to feel that hot sting of awareness strike into her. She couldn't, no matter how she tried, justify it in her own mind. She should hate him, and perhaps she did in a way, but did she have to want him so badly? She didn't like herself much for feeling as she did. In fact, she found her own desires harder to accept than Anton's desire for her. He was a man, after all, and, as all women knew, their sexual needs followed more animalistic paths than a woman's did. So what did that make her? An animal, like him? She shuddered, liking herself even less. She had the awful feeling that was exactly what she was, a sexually woken animal.

The car slowed, and she blinked, snapping forcefully out of her heavy mood when she recognised the driveway they were just turning into. 'Why are you bringing me here?' she demanded sharply.

'So you can do what I said you need to do, and unwind a little away from the constant worry of your father's illness.'

'Here?' God in heaven, she thought, as she stared at the white-rendered mansion house. This is the last place on earth I could wind down in!

'Don't put your imagination on overdrive,' he drawled as he stopped the car. 'I have not brought you here with the exclusive intention of ravishing you.'

The cynical mockery brought an uncomfortable flush to her cheeks, and he smiled tightly at it as he climbed out, striding around the bonnet to open her door, his hand determined as it closed over her elbow to help her alight.

'You know, Nina,' he went on grimly, 'if you could bring yourself to trust me a little, maybe you would find I am not the complete sex maniac you seem to believe me to be.'

She shook her head, and said nothing. How was she supposed to trust him when she couldn't even trust herself? That terrible flow of attraction was already humming between them. And he only held her lightly by the arm!

She heaved in an unsteady breath and let him lead her into the same house which, only a week ago, he had so angrily ejected her from.

'John!' he called out the moment they stepped beyond the curtained vestibule and into the polished warmth of the inner hallway.

The man she remembered seeing him with that same night a week ago appeared in the study doorway, his curious gaze flicking from his employer to Nina then back again.

'Find Mrs Lukas and ask her to prepare a light lunch to eat by the pool,' he ordered briskly. 'Then take the rest of the day off; we won't be doing any work today.' He was pulling Nina along behind him as he spoke, so they had gone past the man called John when Anton added as a mere afterthought, 'Oh, and by the way——' stopping so abruptly that Nina cannoned into him. He caught her gently by the shoulders and turned her around to face the other man. 'This is Nina Lovell, and we will be getting married in three weeks, so I will want you to get on to all the arrangements as soon as you can.' He turned again, either not seeing or arrogantly ignoring two completely stunned expressions. His arm was firm around her shoulders now, clasping her to his side. 'But not today, John!' he called over his shoulder. 'Today I want some peace and quiet to be alone with my fiancée!'

The poor John's muffled, 'Yes, sir' fell on indifferent ears. Anton was already opening a door and guiding Nina through it into a glass-canopied room that made her completely forget the shock announcement he had just made to his assistant.

'Oh!' she gasped, gazing around the luxurious pine room where the sun glinted down through the glass-domed roof on to a large swimming pool. White plastic tables and chairs were dotted in a kind of organised randomness around the pool edge, their seats thickly padded with pale peach, lemon and green-striped cushions. The heavy drizzle of a week ago had been blown away on the fresh breeze now cleaning the summer air outside, making it cool enough to strike a chill into the body, but in here the air was warm and humid, the steam gently rising from the expanse of clean, calm water telling her that it was invitingly heated.

'What better place to unwind than spending a lazy hour here?' Anton claimed. He was already dragging his tie from his throat and shrugging out of his expensive jacket.

His movements drew her eyes to him, and her senses began to stir when she saw how the fine fabric of his shirt had pulled taut across his broad chest, revealing the dark shadowy evidence of what lay beneath, asserting disturbing memories of crisp black chest hair rasping against her searching fingers.

Dry-mouthed, she looked quickly away from him, 'I—I can't swim here,' she said a little breathlessly. 'I haven't brought anything to wear.'

'No problem.' He waved a casual hand to a door across the pool. 'You should find something suitable in there...' He was already moving off towards a matching door on the other side of the pool. 'You have ten minutes to change and join me,' he added smoothly before he disappeared.

She stayed where she was for a moment, wanting to refuse, but not quite finding the courage to do so. It didn't need any special powers to know that he was not prepared to take no for an answer. If she didn't change and join him in the allotted time, he would take steps to make sure she did.

'Damned man,' she muttered to herself as she moved to obey him.

Ten minutes later to the second, she slid shyly out of the changing-room wearing a bright blue one-piece which was the only thing in a veritable store of female swimming gear that she'd considered half decent enough to wear, and even that was too cut away at the thighs for decency, its fine silk lycra fabric clinging to every single curve of her body so she felt almost as naked with it on as she'd felt without it.

Anton was already in the pool, pounding up and down with the brisk smooth strokes of the born swimmer, his brief white trunks doing little to soothe her fevered imagination. His skin was bronze and slick, muscles rippling as he cut a clean line through the water. Chewing uncertainly on her bottom lip, she lowered herself carefully down the steps and into the pleasantly warm water, relieved to get under out of sight before he realised she was there.

He powered up the pool towards her, dark head lifting on every other stroke so he could draw breath. She watched him in breathless awe, envious of his style, of his air of easy elegance, even in such a casual situation. His hand touched the end of the pool and up came his head, water cascading down his face as his eyes arrowed right on her, and she went still, waiting for she knew not what, then he grinned, did a neat rolling turn and powered away again leaving her wilting with relief.

It took time, but eventually she began to relax, mainly because he took no more notice of her after that one quick grin, and she swam more leisurely around the pool, feeling the slow erosion of her tension, and even managing to smile at it in the end. Anton had promised no seduction, and he obviously meant it.

She was floating lazily on her back when he eventually came up beside her. The sun was glinting down through the overhead glass dome, and she had her eyes closed, but at the light touch of his hand on her cheek her lids flicked open to glance warily at him.

'You are feeling a little more relaxed?' he enquired.

She nodded, feeling foolish for her strange mood earlier, and she told him so shyly.

His eyes were thoughtful, giving little away of himself. 'You have been under a great strain,' he made excuse for her.

Nina just smiled. She was still under a great strain, but instead of her father being the cause of it this man was, this dark and frighteningly attractive man who could raise goose-bumps on her skin just by looking at her.

'We all have to find time to relax and play, Nina,' he said after a moment. Then he grinned, perfectly square white teeth flashing in a suddenly satirically mocking face. 'Even I—wicked devil that I am in your eyes—like to take time off to play!'

She couldn't help it—she laughed too, the light sound pealing delicately in the high-domed room.

'That's better,' he murmured in wry satisfaction. 'I was beginning to wonder if you knew how to smile.'

'The same could be said of you,' she said, blushing a little.

'Yes,' he sombrely agreed. 'Ours has been a grim association until now.' Then, just as the mood threatened to grow heavy on them, he was smiling again, and reaching out to capture one of her hands, laying its palm flat on top of his own. 'See how pearly white your skin looks next to mine,' he mockingly observed, 'It looks almost as though your poor skin has never been exposed to the sun.'

Her stomach did a somersault and she dropped her legs, pulling her hand away as she trod water beside him, eyes making an involuntary sweep of his beautifully tanned body. 'Only because you Greeks are a race of thankless sun worshippers,' she answered scornfully, happy to continue the playful mood. 'While I have far more absorbing things to do with my time!'

With a resounding splash, she hit the water just by his face, then dived off, laughing as he spluttered beneath the surface in surprise.

She was just pushing herself out of the pool when he caught her, dragging her back by the waist and twisting her around to face him, his strong arms wrapping right around her in an effort to hold on to her slippery figure.

'Don't you dare kiss me!' she shrieked, seeing the intention in his gaze when he turned her around to face him, and rueing her own recklessness in daring to tease this man of all men.

'Why not?' His voice was full of lazy amusement. 'This is my pool, my water, and you are my own personal water nymph. I caught you, so I can kiss you whenever I want to!'

His feet were planted firmly on the pool bottom, but Nina's didn't reach, making her reliant on his grip on her to keep her head above water, and her hands went to clutch at his shoulders, fingers splaying out across the cool wet silk of his skin. Her gaze was drawn to the sleek cord of muscle where his shoulder met his neck, and her mouth went dry when she saw the darkened line which was all that was left of the wound she had inflicted on him over a week ago.

The sudden urge to place her lips against the mark had her heart clamouring wildly in her breast. 'Please let me go, Anton,' she pleaded breathlessly, panicked by her own feelings.

'No.' He shook his head, still amused, this lighter-hearted and playful man just as dangerous as the sexually hungry one she was used to seeing. 'Kiss or forfeit for splashing me,' he offered generously. 'You choose.'

'I...' The pink tip of her tongue threaded nervously around her lips. It was a kiss or a ducking, she realised that, and she had to choose the forfeit of course; even he was expecting her to. But the kiss was suddenly a real temptation. His mouth was very close to her own, so close she only had to move a fraction to... 'Forfeit!' she cried out in outright denial of her own traitorous desires.

'Too late,' he murmured, and did what she had been aching to do, and closed the gap between their hungry mouths.

It was fascinating, this feeling of weightlessness on the outside with the water lapping around her shoulders, and the weightlessness on the inside with the deep drugging sensuality of the kiss. Anton drew her closer, her long legs automatically tangling with his beneath the clear surface of the water. She could feel the texture of his hair-roughened limbs chafing pleasantly against her own, and her toes curled, the soft padded soles of her feet sliding delicately along his legs.

His arms tightened around her. 'Open your mouth,' he commanded huskily.

'No,' she refused, then melted anyway, bringing a warm laugh bubbling up from his chest as he acknowledged her easy surrender.

Then there was no laughter, no playfulness in the game whatsoever as the mood flipped over from the passive to the passionate, and the kiss was deepened by a mutual desire that sent them both straining desperately against each other.

'Well, well, well,' a thick-as-cream voice drawled from somewhere above them. 'This is—nice.'

If anything had the power to bring them both clattering back to a sense of the present, then that voice did. Nina froze in his arms, feeling at the same time Anton stiffen just before he slowly withdrew his mouth from hers.

'Fate seems determined to spoil our more—pleasurable moments, *matia mou*,' he murmured drily, sighing his dissatisfaction as Nina hid her hot face in his throat.

'Hello, Louisa,' he said. He didn't look up, keeping Nina against him, his mouth sliding lazily across her heated cheek, playing sensuously with her as if the other woman's unexpected appearance altered nothing. 'This is a—surprise.'

He wasn't being nice, and both women knew it. Nina pushed at his shoulders, her embarrassment total when he pressed a final clinging kiss to her lips before giving in to the pressure of her hands. But only in so far as to transfer his own hands to the tiled edge of the pool, effectively trapping her against the pool wall and the rigid planes of his richly tanned body.

'Let me go,' she whispered uncomfortably. She couldn't look up; she was just too aware of the other woman standing directly above them, appalled at what she must have witnessed—appalled at her own wanton behaviour. They had been so engrossed in each other that they hadn't even heard Louisa enter the pool-room!

'No,' he refused, turning his attention on their intruder. 'I did think I had given orders not to be disturbed, but...' a long sigh left him, lifting the black shadowed expanse of his bronzed chest then letting it fall again in a way that held Nina's breath locked tightly in her throat '...I must have been mistaken.'

'Oh, you know Mrs Lukas, darling,' Louisa dismissed lightly. 'She knows you never mean me.'

'Is that so?' It was rather like a dangerous cat playing with its equal. 'How stupid of me not to make my meaning clearer.'

'Very.' Louisa agreed. 'Are you going to stay in there much longer, Anton?' she enquired. 'Because, if so, I may as well undress and join you.'

'Not if you value your health, Louisa,' Anton said, and at last slid sideways from Nina so he could lever himself out of the pool, the water cascading down his beautiful body as he went.

'My, but we are being modest today, aren't we?' Nina heard Louisa taunt, dark eyes mocking the brief white swimming trunks he was wearing. 'I haven't seen you wear those in years, Anton, not in years!'

'Do you want slapping, minx?' he threatened, the indulgent use of that pet name stinging Nina's memory. These two were so intimate with each other that it screamed 'lovers'—just as it had done that night she had watched them go into each other's arms!

Anton turned to offer her his hand as an aid to help her out of the water. She didn't want to take it, she would much rather have turned tail and dived beneath the surface out of view of the lovely mocking eyes of Louisa. Yet, and oddly, it was that exact same look which asserted her composure, bringing her chin up, blue eyes hinting at defiance as she accepted Anton's hand and let him haul her easily from the pool.

'Thank you,' she murmured as she landed neatly beside him.

'My pleasure,' he mocked her trite remark. 'Let me introduce you to an—old friend of mine.' For 'old friend' replace 'mistress', Nina thought as a fierce shaft of pure jealousy streaked right through her. 'Nina,' he went on softly, pulling her closer to his side while his bland gaze fixed itself on Louisa's mocking face, 'I would like you to meet a very old friend of the Lakitos family, Louisa Mandraki. Nina Lovell, Louisa,' he continued in that same soft careful tone. 'My future wife.'

There was a stunned silence. Louisa's composure slipped, her magnificent Yves St Laurent frame going as rigid as a pillar of ice as she stared at him.

'You can't mean this, Anton?' she managed to gasp in horrified disbelief.

'A real surprise, is it not?' He deliberately ignored Louisa's horror. 'You are stunned,' he kindly allowed. 'And rightly so. I am rather stunned myself!'

'B-but what about...?' she faltered, lush mouth quivering slightly, and Nina began to wish herself a million miles away. 'Does your mother know about this?'

Mother—what mother? Nina hadn't known he had a mother!

'Of course,' he calmly assured her. 'I informed her personally via the telephone only yesterday, or I would not be telling you now, Louisa,' he oh, so silkily pointed out. 'You know what a stickler for convention my mother is.'

'Yes...' Louisa's gaze narrowed as it slid over to Nina's stiff, uncomfortable face. Her composure was quickly restored. 'May I offer you my congratulations, Miss Lovell?' She lifted a long limp hand towards her, the length of its red-tipped nails so potentially lethal that Nina shuddered.

My God, she thought as she let her own hand slide briefly across Louisa's. She wants to kill me. 'Thank you,' she answered as coolly as she could.

'And you, darling, of course...' The smile she turned on Anton was warm and seductive, lovely face lifting up to him for his kiss.

He let go of Nina so he could oblige, leaving her standing there in seething silence while the two dark heads closed on each other with easy intimacy, the only thing stopping them from folding each other in a real clinch being the fear that the droplets of water still clinging to his hard, bronzed body would spoil Louisa's exquisite designer suit!

By the time he drew away, Louisa's eyes were smiling cat-like into his gleaming black ones. 'I think this calls for champagne, don't you, Anton?' she suggested huskily. 'Why don't you go and see if you have a bottle on ice somewhere while your—fiancée tells me all about your—romance?'

'What a good idea!' He turned back to Nina, laying one of his white-toothed smiles on her as he bent to place a kiss on her unresponsive lips.

Don't you dare leave me alone with her, her eyes warned him. The grin just widened. He was enjoying this, she realised angrily. He thought it all just a huge joke to have his future wife faced with his mistress! 'I'll only be a moment!' he assured her, touching her scorching cheek with a teasing finger, then sauntered off, whistling softly beneath his breath, leaving Nina with the nagging suspicion that he had left the two of them alone like this on purpose, just to see who would still be alive when he got back!

Well, she for one, refused to take the test. 'If you'll excuse me,' she murmured politely, 'I'll go and get changed while...'

'Running away, darling?' the thick-as-cream voice taunted. 'I really can't blame you. It was very naughty of Anton not to tell you about me.'

Nina's chin went up, her wet hair flying across her shoulder as she let her cool blue gaze fix with Louisa's hard black one. 'Oh, I already know all about you, Miss Mandraki,' she said sweetly. 'You are Anton's—old friend.'

'My dear girl.' Louisa's smile was full of humiliating mockery. 'There is a lot more between us than just a mere friendship.'

'That's—very nice,' Nina remarked insipidly, refusing to bite the bait, even while she was a seething mass of antagonism inside.

'His mother will not accept you, you know,' she was told. 'Ianthe has strict ideals where her only son is concerned. She does not believe in mixing the races. A Greek wife is the only kind of woman she will welcome into her family, and Anton knows it, which...' she paused to look curiously at Nina '...which only makes this—announcement of his all the more intriguing...'

If she wanted to make Nina feel even more uncomfortable with this marriage idea, then she was succeeding. The daunting prospect of having to face a hostile mother-in-law did not appeal at all. 'I won't be marrying his mother,' she said, keeping her expression cool with effort.

'You won't be marrying her son, either, if Ianthe has anything to do with it,' Louisa stated with calm certainty. 'Lovell...' she then murmured thoughtfully, sending her narrowed gaze on a crucifying scan of Nina's scantily clad figure. 'Lovell ... now why does that name ring a shrill bell inside my head ... ?' The black eyes studied Nina's proudly defiant face for a moment, then a sly smile ruined the lush contours of her mouth. 'Ah, yes. It is Jonas Lovell's company which owns several properties in central London, is it not?' she mused silkily. 'The ones Anton has been trying to get his hands on for several months now, unless I am mistaken ...'

No, you're not mistaken, Nina thought heavily as the silky observation hung in the air between them, making Nina look away and Louisa's smile widen as she noted her reaction.

'I wonder if knowing that will make you more acceptable to Ianthe?' Louisa went on curiously. 'We Greeks are all for marriages of expediency. And you never know, several million pounds' worth of good development land may just swing things in your favour—but what does it feel like, Miss Lovell,' she then taunted softly, 'to know yourself bought and sold like that?'

'Now wait a minute ...' Stung by the damning truth in the words, Nina's chin came up. 'You have no right to——'

'I have every right!' Louisa cut in, and suddenly the silk gloves were off, revealing the furiously angry woman beneath. 'Anton is mine, do you hear?' She took a threatening step towards Nina, her stilettoed shoes screeching on the tiled pool-room floor. 'He has always been mine! We have been lovers for years!'

'Which makes you—what exactly?' Nina found it in her to taunt right back.

Louisa went pale. 'If you believe he will stop coming to me just because he marries himself to you, then you are a fool!' Her lush mouth turned down in a sneer. 'You, with your cold English passion, what do you have that will stop a man like Anton Lakitos straying back to more—satisfying favours?'

Blue eyes flashed their contempt for Louisa and all she stood for. 'Virginity, Miss Mandraki,' she heard herself reply, and was almost as shocked as Louisa at hearing it. 'Isn't that as precious to a Greek as the property you say I shall bring with me into our marriage?' Louisa couldn't know it, but the words were hurting Nina to say as much as they were hurting the Greek woman to hear. 'Surely,' she pressed her point scathingly home, 'even his high-principled mother will see the asset in having a daughter-in-law who hasn't *been around*, as we cold English like to call it!'

A direct hit, Nina noted as the beautiful Grecian face contorted, dark eyes flashing a single warning at her just before rage transformed itself into action, and Nina shied jerkily away as a beautifully manicured hand came winging out towards her face.

She landed in the pool with more urgency than grace, her heart pounding in frantic response to the distasteful scene she had just endured, followed by the eruption of violence. Her own quick reactions were the only things which had saved her from the vicious swipe from Louisa's red-tipped nails, and she swam away beneath the water, staying submerged for as long as she could, listening to the angry click of Louisa's feet echoing in the water, and praying that the terrible woman was leaving and not intending jumping in after her.

'My God,' she gasped when eventually her bursting lungs insisted she come up for air.

'Greek women are renowned for their shocking tempers,' a smooth voice drawled.

Nina spun around in the water. Anton was leaning against the pool-room door, an ice bucket containing a bottle of champagne tucked into the crook of his arm.

Her eyes spat angry fire at him. 'How much of that did you hear?' she demanded.

'Not much, I am sorry to say.' He looked disappointed. 'But by the look on Louisa's face as she pushed by me just now I would say you must have come out on top. Well done,' he dipped his dark head in sardonic applause, then spoiled it by adding balefully, 'Though I think it will now take some careful pampering on my behalf to bring her back into good humour.'

'Well.' She turned away from him in disgust. 'I'm getting out of here,' she told him angrily. 'Before any more of your—women arrive to stake their claim!' Swimming to the side of the pool, she pulled herself out of the water, her wet hair lying in a thick pelt down her back as she walked angrily towards the door he was so arrogantly propped up against.

'This annoying habit you have of leaving my home only half dressed will have to be curbed, Nina, my love,' he drawled lazily, the infuriating humour in his voice bringing her to a skidding halt so that she could glare at him—only to wish she hadn't when she caught the way his appreciative gaze was running freely over her. 'Only, I can't have my wife flaunting her...' the eyes did another run of her body '...charms for all and sundry to see.'

'I am not your wife yet!' she snapped, cheeks running hot with colour as she swung away again, making this time for the changing-room where she had left her clothes, furiously aware how well she deserved the taunt because that had been exactly what she had been intending to do: to walk out of here wearing only a skimpy blue bathing suit!

'Need any help?' he offered maddeningly.

'Go to hell!' she snarled and slammed the changing-room door shut.

CHAPTER SIX

WHEN Nina came out again, Anton was sitting by the poolside waiting for her. He was dressed again, and looking just the same as he had when he'd arrived at her home that morning. Only the sleek dampness of his hair said that he had been doing anything other than sitting at his desk working all day. Nina's mouth went dry as she looked at him, and she damned the dryness just as she damned the way her heart fluttered at the mere sight of him.

'You are lovers,' she accused, keeping the full width of the pool between them.

'Louisa and I are a lot of things to each other,' he answered smoothly.

'As I've said before, you're despicable.'

Dark brows rose at her. 'How does it feel,' he enquired, 'to desire such a despicable fellow as me?'

The taunt hit home, heating her cheeks and closing her throat in despair. He was right. She did desire him, even while she hated the very sight of him. 'I would like to go home now, please,' she informed him primly.

'I am sure you would,' he agreed. 'But not yet. Not until you've sat down here and eaten something.' He waved a hand towards a loaded tray his housekeeper must have brought in while Nina was changing. 'We need to talk, you and I, and you are too thin. I would go as far as to say that you have lost almost a stone in weight since the first time I saw you.'

He could actually remember back that far back with so many women passing through his life? Nina was derisively surprised. She stayed where she was, eyeing him uncertainly, wondering if she dared defy him and just walk right out of here. She'd had enough of Anton Lakitos for one day!

'If I have to come and fetch you, you won't like it.'

He reads minds too, she grumbled to herself as lack of courage sent her around the pool to sit down opposite him, selecting a sandwich with a churlishness that only made him smile at her as though she were a silly child which, in turn, sent the resentment deeper.

The sandwich was surprisingly good though, she allowed, sinking her teeth into fresh salmon and finely chopped celery, keeping her eyes firmly averted from him while he seemed content to sip at his black coffee, prepared to stretch the tension between them out to breaking point before he began his threatened 'talk'.

She took another sandwich.

'Have you heard anything from Hunter since last week?'

Nina went still, the sandwich hovering halfway to her mouth. Obviously, he wasn't going to stretch it out. 'No,' she answered, her heart slowing to a heavy thump at the outright lie. He couldn't know about Jason's letters—could he? she told herself. She had thrown them all away. 'Did you "pay him off" as you promised to do?' she felt confident enough to throw right back.

He ignored the taunt. 'I am sure you have considered the consequences if I ever find out that you are lying to me,' he warned her levelly.

Nina lifted curious blue eyes to his. 'And will you inform me of any contact you have with the lovely Louisa from now on?' she asked, and her small white teeth closed over the sandwich.

He smiled at that. 'Are you sure you want to know?' he drawled. 'I saw the green devils glinting in your eyes earlier. Jealousy has a way of clouding the truth, and the truth of the matter is, I can't promise no contact with Louisa because we do—business together from time to time.'

'Don't forget the family connection,' she reminded him, not believing him for a minute. He had no intention of staying away from the lovely Louisa. She was enough to knock any man's eyes out.

'As you say,' he seemed happy to agree. 'She is also the daughter of my mother's best friend. Whereas your Jason has no excuse whatsoever to get in touch with you.'

'Except our music,' Nina put in, taking another sandwich and biting eagerly into it. The swim had made her hungry, or maybe it was the kisses—no, she dismissed that thought with an angry toss of her head. 'Jason and I belong to the same music group,' she explained, glad to have something to annoy him with. 'So we are bound to meet once—' she gave a careless shrug '—maybe twice a week.'

'Which brings me nicely on to another—rather delicate subject,' he said quietly, and Nina felt her nerves tingle to the surface of her skin. She wasn't going to like what was coming next, she was sure of it. 'Your college education.'

Nina put aside the sandwich, her suspicions confirmed. 'What about it?' she said warily. 'I begin a new term in October, that shouldn't be any——' She fell into a choking silence. He was already shaking his head, his meaning so horribly clear that her heart dropped to her stomach. 'No!' She refused to believe what her suspicions were saying to her, stretching out a hand as if to ward him off. 'You can't mean it. You can't really mean to take my music away from me.'

He caught the hand, holding it tightly in his own. 'You have to understand,' he urged her. 'It will be impossible for you to continue once we are married.' He was sorry; there was genuine sorrow in his voice as he said it. 'I travel a lot, I will expect you to travel with me. We will be man and wife in every facet of the union, Nina. I want you beside me in whatever bed it is I have to sleep in!'

'No.' She rose shakily to her feet, her hand still caught in his, the fingers cold and trembling. 'I won't give up my studies for you. I'll live here in your home with y-you. Be w-whatever it is,' she swallowed thickly, 'it is you want me to be to you, here, while in this house! But I won't throw away years of study because you are Greek enough to believe your wife's only place in life is to be stuck to your side!'

'I entertain a lot,' he persisted. 'You will naturally be my hostess—whatever country I happen to be in. I want and expect you to take up that role.' Dark eyes took on a hard immovable cast. 'There will be no time for your college studies, Nina. I am sorry, but there it is.'

'No.' The quickly drying tumble of glorious red hair trembled as she shook her head. 'No, I refuse to agree to it.'

He stared grimly at her for a moment, studying the set contours of her mouth, the angry heat in her cheeks, and the determined tilt of her small chin. Then something flickered across his face, the merest hint of pain, or was it irritation? Whatever, he sat back suddenly, releasing her hand as though it repulsed him, and the new look on his face was pure irony which seemed, oddly, to be aimed entirely at himself.

Then he said, quite flatly, 'I am not really giving you any choice, you know,' and watched, without any feeling whatsoever, all the colour drain from her face.

He had to be bluffing, she was thinking hectically. He wasn't that rotten, surely? He was just trying to put the fear of God into her for some reason, that was all, force her to acknowledge who had control over their——

'Of course,' he continued when she hadn't managed to utter a single word in response, 'if your music is worth more to you than trying to build a successful marriage with me, then by all means forget the marriage and go chase your rainbows. What right have I to deny you? But,' he added silkily, 'are those rainbows worth more to you than your father's health and happiness?'

'I'll give up my studies!' she choked, sitting down with a bump, beaten, as always, beaten by his more ruthless will.

He should have been triumphant, when all he looked was bitterly cynical. 'So, you will fight me to the death if I beg you to accept something on my behalf alone,' he jeered. 'But as soon as your father and his precious company is mentioned, you surrender without a second thought!'

'That is what this is all about, isn't it?' she choked, hating him with the pained blue of her eyes. 'My father and his company—or I wouldn't be sitting here with you at all!'

'That is certainly the truth,' he muttered. Then, without any warning, he leapt forwards in his chair, his hand snaking out to slam down on top of hers where it lay trembling on the plastic table-top, making her jump in surprise and the tray of fine crockery rattle dangerously, and Nina found herself looking at the frighteningly angry man she had always known lurked just beneath the surface of that urbane mask he liked to wear.

'So, now we will have the full truth,' he demanded gruffly. 'And you will tell me all about those secret love-letters you have been receiving from your darling Jason!'

Her eyes went wide in horror. 'You know about the letters?' she breathed.

'I know about the damned letters,' he scathingly confirmed. 'You will not be given the chance to cheat on me with Hunter,' he bit out grimly. 'No woman makes a fool out of me—especially one who is such a consummate liar as you have just proved yourself to be! Or one I know already has a penchant for sneaking into other men's bedrooms when the mood takes her!'

'That's not fair!' she jumped to her own defence. 'When I came to your room that night, it wasn't to...'

'Seduce me?' he offered when her own throat clammed up on the word. 'But how do I know that?' The black eyes were cynically mocking. 'You may have been planning all along to—place me in a compromising situation so you could blackmail me into leaving Lovell's alone. Or you would ruin my reputation by telling the world how I was capable of seducing a sick man's daughter at the same time as I stole his company from under him!'

It hit her then, just what was going on here, and she sighed, sitting back in her seat in much the same way he had done earlier. 'You actually read my letters from Jason,' she flatly accused, trying to recall just how Jason had worded it.

> We could threaten to tell the world how he blackmailed you into letting him seduce you. Think how much he would be prepared to pay to squash that kind of slur on his character. In the speculator business, a man relies on his social contacts to keep him in the know. He would become a social pariah if it ever got out that he was capable of seducing a sick man's daughter at the same time as he stole his company away from him. With a bit of clever planning, we could make him pay enough to put Lovell's back on an even keel again, then your father could do nothing else but accept me, and be grateful that we'd plucked him out of Lakitos's greedy clutches.

'How did you get hold of them?' she asked now, turning dulled blue eyes on him.

His shrug was pure indifference. 'I fished them out of the waste-paper basket.'

Of course, she thought. How stupid of her. He had used her father's study every morning—after she had used it to read Jason's letters before discarding them. How utterly stupid of her not to guess that he would be arrogant enough to retrieve and read them.

'Jason wrote a lot of lies in those letters, Anton,' she murmured huskily. 'He was talking wildly, and I didn't want you misinterpreting his meaning.' It was his own pain and confusion that had made Jason write what he had. He just could not come to terms with the fact that it was over between them.

'And which, in your opinion, were the lies, and which the truth?' he enquired cynically. 'Perhaps all his insinuations about me were the truth—or were they lies? Or maybe the intensity of his love for you was the truth—or was that a lie also?' Nina wriggled uncomfortably where she sat, and he leaned forwards suddenly, grasping her chin between a hard finger and thumb, forcing her to look at him. 'And what about all those—emotive pleas to meet with you, Nina?' he demanded roughly. 'Were they just wishful thinking on his part, or have you actually been meeting with him behind my back?'

The finger and thumb pinched painfully, and Nina set her mouth tightly shut in outright refusal to answer him. Sparking blue eyes warred with burning black, and the air around them began to buzz, with anger, with disdain, and with that forever present sexual turmoil that always complicated any issue they took up with each other.

'Have you been meeting with him?' The hard black eyes demanded an answer.

'Why, are you by any chance jealous?' she threw back tartly, then sat watching in wide-eyed fascination as two streaks of revealing colour whipped across his high cheekbones. He *was* jealous, she realised, as her senses clamoured in hectic triumph at the discovery.

'Bitch!' he breathed out hoarsely, hating her for surprising that piece of truth out of him. 'You damned beautiful bitch!' Her triumph was very short-lived as he yanked her mouth on to his, using the cruelty of his finger and thumb to do it, and punishing her mouth with a fury that pulsed frighteningly between them.

By the time they broke apart, they were both struggling for breath, gasping on the excitement of a hot and hated sensuality.

'Now you will tell me what I want to know,' he insisted huskily.

'Why should I tell you anything?' she muttered, lifting trembling fingers to the tender flesh of her bruised mouth. 'You want to take everything away from me, yet give nothing back in return!' She wouldn't cry, she would not! 'As long as you deprive me of my college studies, I won't tell you anything I don't want to!'

The anger left him, replaced with a grim resolve which showed no hint of softness anywhere, 'You can play your piano in our home until my ears ring with the sound of it, Nina. But you will not be returning to college after the summer recess.'

'But Jason doesn't even attend the college!' she burst out wretchedly. 'Only the music group. I'll give that up!' she promised eagerly. 'I'll——' the uncompromising set of his jaw slewed her to a thudding stop. 'Oh, God,' she choked, and buried her face in her hands, wondering painfully if there was anything left for him to do to her.

'Come on,' he sighed, sounding as beaten as she felt. 'I'll take you home.'

The journey was not a happy one. Neither of them spoke; it all seemed to have been well and truly said. When he drew the car to a halt outside her home, Nina was relieved that he didn't switch off the car engine. It meant he wasn't coming in.

'I have to go away for a few days,' he informed her. 'John Calver, my assistant, will be in contact with you about the wedding arrangements. Leave everything to him.' An order, not negotiable. 'All you have to do before we marry is buy yourself a gown which will do honour to us both.'

'Black,' she mumbled bitterly. 'Mourning black to match my——'

'Listen to me, you aggravating fool!' he snarled, making her blink as he pushed his angry face close up to hers. 'Remember just who all this is being done for! And if that doesn't help seal your vicious tongue, then try remembering this!' His hand snaked out to grip her nape. 'I only have to touch you like this——' his mouth landed on top of her own, driving the breath from her body and the will to fight him from her soul as he kissed her with such agonising thoroughness that she was whimpering by the time he dragged his lips away '—to have you aching for more of the same!' he finished as if the long passionate gap in the middle hadn't been there.

'I wish I had never set eyes on you!' she choked, shamefully aware of how her throbbing lips burned for his to plunder them once again.

'The feeling is entirely mutual,' he gratingly agreed. 'I cannot think of anything less palatable than marrying myself to a crazy, mixed-up child who does not know when to curb her impulsive tongue!'

'Then why are you?' she cried in bitter challenge.

Black eyes flashed across her strained face. 'You know why,' he growled. 'Because I can hardly keep my hands off that responsive little body of yours.'

'You don't have to marry me to do that,' she pointed out wearily. 'You are in the position of calling all the shots—are still calling them!' She turned her face away from the grim hard cast of his. 'Haven't I already proved to you that I'll do anything to make my father happy?'

'Then be glad I am prepared to marry you to get what I want,' he snapped, then sighed heavily. 'Go inside, Nina,' he advised. 'Before this really degenerates into the slanging match you seem intent on. And Nina,' he added as she went to scramble quickly from the car, 'remember with whom your loyalty now lies.' He grimly warned, 'Hunter is in your past, and in the past is where I intend to keep him. No more lies. I want to know if he so much as sends you a postcard, got that?'

'Yes.' She'd got it. She now belonged to Anton Lakitos. Bought, body and aching soul.

He was away almost a week, and it was a week when she didn't know what was worse: having him around to constantly remind her why she was letting herself be coerced like this, or not having him around so her mind could work overtime conjuring up all kinds of horrors that could befall her under his uncaring hands.

In the end, she went to her piano to search of escape, and found it in the complicated absorption of teaching herself a new Mozart piece.

'That was nice to hear,' her father said when she entered his room later that day. He had been improving steadily, and was now allowed to sit in the chair beside his bed, though he spent most of his time there dozing. 'I hadn't realised how much I'd missed hearing you play until today.'

'I haven't felt much like playing while you've been so ill,' she explained her neglect of the piano, then smiled a little wanly. 'Anton doesn't want me to continue my studies after we're married,' she confessed sadly.

Her father glanced sharply at her. 'I guessed he might feel that way,' he said gruffly. 'He loves you,' he smiled as if that said it all, and Nina wanted to weep. 'And these Greek fellows can be damned possessive of their women. Give him a few children,' he advised. 'That'll soothe his ego a little. Then, if you still want to, maybe you can convince him to let you return to your studies.'

She sent him a jaundiced look. 'Do you male chauvinists always stick together?'

'There can be as much self-fulfilment in being a wife and mother as there can be in academic achievement, Nina,' he said carefully. 'Don't let the feminists' view brainwash you into believing yourself only half a woman because you've chosen love and marriage to a good man over your career.'

Love, she thought heavily. What was love? Perhaps, if love were there between herself and Anton, she could accept any sacrifice she would be forced to make.

'And think how it would gladden your old papa's heart to bounce his grandson on his knee,' Jonas added, blue eyes glinting with their old foxiness again after weeks of being so dull and lifeless that Nina didn't have the heart to douse the light with the cutting reply that naturally jumped to her lips.

But she wasn't above putting in her own little dig. 'So you don't mind the father of your grandson being the man you once hated enough to murder?'

'That was all a—misunderstanding,' he huffed out dismissively, his face closing up on her as it always did when she tried to discuss his relationship with Anton. 'I—I owed him money, you know,' he added suddenly.

'Yes.' Nina nodded. 'Anton told me.'

'He did?' Jonas looked surprised, then added defensively, 'I could have paid him back if the old ticker hadn't gone on the blink!'

'I'm sure you could,' Nina allowed, not sure of it at all.

'But, as it is,' he murmured tiredly, leaning back in his seat and closing his eyes, 'I can rest easier knowing he's taking care of Lovell's. There are a lot of sharks out there, Nina, waiting to pounce on a sick old man like me; Anton was only one of them. At least, now you're marrying him, I'll always know that everything I've worked for through the years will stay in the family. It's a good feeling, that.' He sighed with satisfaction, then peered slyly at her through the narrowed slits of his lowered lids. 'Just do your part, and make sure of that grandson I need to inherit. Then this old man can die contented.'

Could you see it? Nina leaned closer to her dressing mirror to peer at her own reflection. No, her smile was lopsided and faintly cynical. You couldn't actually see the rope being slowly tightened around her neck, pulled steadily by her father on one end and Anton on the other. It didn't show; it was an invisible noose.

It was Saturday evening, and Anton was due to come and collect her in a few minutes. She had received the royal summons, as she mocked John Calver's telephone call of yesterday. Anton was apparently arriving from

Greece today, and would be bringing his mother to meet her.

She was invited for dinner.

What a treat, she grimly mocked. I am to be looked over to see if I come up to the high standards his mother apparently has for her son's bride. Well, there was one thing for certain, she knew as she applied a final touch of blusher to her too-pale cheeks: not even the daunting Ianthe could fault her appearance tonight; she had spent too many long painstaking hours making sure of it.

Nevertheless, there was a definite lump of nervous tension in her throat as she stood up to view the finished effects in the long mirror. Her gown was a long, sleek, knitted silk thing that covered her from throat to wrist to ankle except for the upside-down heart-shape cut out of the bodice just above the rounded slopes of her breasts. She had bought it to wear to one of her father's formal receptions because its elegantly classical lines had the courage-lifting effect of adding years to her paltry twenty, putting her more on a par with the kind of highly sophisticated women who usually attended those affairs. The shimmering turquoise colour of the silk echoed the blue of her eyes and reacted beautifully with the rich red colour of her hair, caught up tonight in a smooth coroneted pleat. And the whole effect held a certain dignity about it which went a little way to soothing her hectic nerves.

It was also the dress she had been wearing the first time Anton had seen her, she reminded herself as she turned away to collect her wrap and purse. But that didn't mean anything—she dismissed the sudden tingling low in her stomach. She hadn't chosen to wear it for that reason, but because it was the dress she felt most confident in.

With a firm lifting of her chin, she walked out of her room and across the landing to say goodnight to her father.

Anton arrived on time, looking so terribly handsome in full black tuxedo that her breath caught in her throat.

His hooded gaze glinted over her, giving nothing away.

'You wear no jewellery,' was his only personal comment, and Nina felt instantly deflated.

'No,' she answered defensively. 'I don't particularly like wearing it.'

A black brow rose in faint mockery. 'Then I hope you learn to like wearing this...' He stepped forward, and instantly her senses were reacting to his sudden closeness. His hand slid into his jacket pocket and came out with a high-domed box which he flicked open with his thumb, and Nina couldn't hold back the gasp of surprise as a huge blue sapphire circled with tiny diamonds winked richly up at her. 'Give me your hand,' he commanded gruffly.

'I...' She touched her dry lips with the moist tip of her tongue. 'Are you sure it is necessary to——?'

'Very sure.' He reached down to capture her left hand when she made no move to offer it to him. 'This ring belonged to my grandmother,' he informed her as he slid the beautiful thing over her slender knuckle. 'My mother will expect to see it on your finger. It was left to me for just such a purpose.'

'I... Thank you,' she whispered, feeling oddly like weeping.

He smiled a little grimly, then did a strange thing, bending his dark head over her hand and pressing his lips against the ring. When he straightened, he didn't look at her, but Nina caught a brief glimpse of something intensely moving on his face before he quashed it, and wondered at it as he led her out to the waiting car.

They were to be chauffeur-driven tonight, she saw as Anton helped her into the back of a long black limousine where the driver sat hidden behind a sheet of obscure glass. 'I am probably a trifle jet lagged,' he explained his reason for the chauffeured car. 'And not really fit to drive myself.'

'I—I thought you had been with your mother in Greece,' she remarked shyly, feeling a little overpowered by the man and the ring glowing deep, deep blue on her finger. 'People don't usually suffer jet lag on such a short plane journey.

'I was in Greece this morning,' he agreed. 'But before that I was in the States, and only stopped off in Athens long enough to collect my mother to escort her to London. I have been continent-hopping,' he informed her sardonically, watching her. She could feel the heat of his gaze on her, though she refused to look back at him. 'Trying to fit two months' work into just a few days.'

'And how...?' Her fingers twisted together as a sign of tension. 'How is your mother taking the news about me?'

Her anxiety had shown in the husky quality of her voice, and Anton was silent for a moment as he studied her. 'She isn't an ogre, you know,' he murmured drily at last.

'No?' She sent him a thin smile that barely touched the edges of her tense mouth. 'Her son is. He must have inherited it from somewhere.'

He laughed softly, shaking his head in rueful appreciation of the little thrust. 'Subdued but not dead, I see,' he drawled. 'Poor unfortunate darling...' he taunted softly. 'You look like Joan of Arc, going bravely to her fate.'

Nina shifted restlessly where she sat, disturbed that he should make such an assessment of her plight.

'I wonder,' he then added musingly, 'if, with hindsight, Mademoiselle d'Arc thought the cause worthy of the sacrifice?'

'How is my father's company doing since you took over its affairs?' she got in her own little dig. Anton might have drawn back from actually taking over the company, but he dealt personally with all Lovell's business affairs now.

'A lot better than it had been doing,' he answered quite seriously. 'No company worth its salt could afford to fritter away its assets as Lovell's had been doing. Heard from Hunter while I've been away?' It was his turn to change the subject, and make her stiffen at the same time.

'No,' she answered stiffly, and it was the truth this time; Jason's letters had stopped abruptly. She levelled him with a suspicious look. 'I suppose you threatened him or something,' she accused.

'I—advised him it would be better if he let sleeping dogs lie from now on,' he amended carefully.

'Same thing,' she said, turning a stony profile on him. 'Whatever, you won't have been nice about it. You don't know how to be.'

'Oh, come here!' he sighed impatiently, taking her completely by surprise when his hand snaked across the gap separating them and pulled her ungently towards him. 'Enough is enough, Nina,' he muttered as he settled her into the warm crook of his arm. 'Your fighting spirit is to be admired, and, God knows, I enjoy sparring with you. It puts such an enchanting light in your beautiful blue eyes. But I am tired,' he sighed, dark eyes roaming her pale and anxious face, 'and in no mood for any of it tonight.'

'Then let me go, and I'll be as quiet as a mouse,' she promised, already having to quell her clamouring pulses.

'What you need is kissing into a better humour,' he stated huskily. 'And I need this, quite desperately in fact,' he groaned as his mouth came slowly down to hers.

The colour was running high in her cheeks by the time he released her, the glow in her eyes easily outshining the bright glitter of precious stone she wore on her finger. With her lips still parted and trembling invitingly, Anton took his time taking it all in, holding the tension like fierce static around them while Nina waited, praying he wouldn't kiss her again—and hoping achingly that he would.

'Just hold that look, *agapi mou*,' he murmured after a while. 'We are almost at my home, and this is exactly how I wish my mother to see you.'

'You did it on purpose!' she cried, sitting bolt upright and hating him all over again.

'Not entirely,' he denied, settling himself comfortably into the corner of the car so he could continue his unnerving study of her at his leisure. 'Five days without you, Nina, is long enough for any normal man to endure, but for one whose desires run as deeply as mine, those five days have been utter purgatory!'

'My God,' she choked, 'You are——'

'Despicable, I know,' he sighed. 'You have told me so often that I am now bored with hearing it. But just remember this, my scratchy little kitten.' His hand found her chin and turned it around to face him. 'My mother is about as innocent as anyone in all of this, so keep your claws sheathed in her company, or I may have to take drastic steps to make sure you do.'

'Threats again, Anton?' she taunted recklessly.

'You had better believe it, Nina,' he confirmed. 'You play the besotted bride, or else. Got that?'

'Yes,' she whispered, the defiance dying as quickly as it had risen. 'I had no intention of doing anything else.'

'Good,' he said, letting go of her. 'We are here.'

CHAPTER SEVEN

'GOOD evening, Miss Lovell.' John Calver was waiting for them as they entered the house, and, after his polite greeting for Nina, he turned an apologetic look on his employer. 'I'm sorry to waylay you just as you've arrived, Anton, but that call from New York you've been expecting has just come through.'

'Damn their lousy timing,' Anton cursed, his eyes warming as they turned on Nina, taking in the lovely picture she made in her deep turquoise gown against a backcloth of richly polished wood. 'I have to speak to them,' he told her huskily.

Nina nodded, unable to manage more than that over the nervous tension she was suffering.

'Where is my mother?' Anton asked John Calver.

'In the drawing-room,' he was informed.

'Then tell New York I will be a few minutes.' He reached out to take the fine silk matching wrap from Nina's shoulders and handed it to his assistant, his dark gaze concentrated on her in a way that had her heart beating shallowly in her breast. How could it be, she wondered achingly, that she could hate this man so furiously, yet want him so badly?

'All right?' he enquired as he drew her towards the door she had once watched people coming and going from one dark and fateful night not so very long ago.

She swallowed. 'Yes,' she said, and lifted her chin.

His soft laughter said he'd noted the mental arming. 'Don't worry,' he soothed as he opened the door. 'My mother is going to love you. How could she not when you look so enchantingly beautiful tonight?'

The compliment flushed the colour back into her cheeks, and Anton smiled his satisfaction as he took them both over the threshold into his mother's presence.

It was a lovely room, was Nina's first hazy thought, the furnishings classically European in shades of pale ivory and gold. She managed to gain an impression of contained luxury and quiet elegance before Anton was demanding her full attention, and drawing her towards the woman just rising from a long ivory sofa.

And immediately Nina's heart sank. She was a woman of formidable presence, tall and strong-boned with the expected jet-black hair swept away from her beautifully preserved olive-skinned face—a face which bore no welcome in its cold black eyes whatsoever.

'Mother,' Anton greeted her warmly, his hand transferring itself to Nina's slender waist as he bent to accept his mother's kiss. 'The New York call I have been expecting has just come through. So I am going to have to make rushed introductions then leave you both to get to know each other. Nina?' He drew her forwards. 'Darling,' he murmured, 'this is my mother. Mother, this is the beautiful creature who has delighted me by promising to be my wife!'

Triumph or challenge? Nina wondered at the emphasised tone in his voice, 'Good evening, Mrs Lakitos,' she greeted her nervously, holding out a decidedly shaky hand, then shivered at the pair of frigid black eyes that turned on her.

'Miss Lovell,' Ianthe Lakitos said formally, ignoring the outstretched hand, but stepping forwards instead to brush her lightly perfumed cheek against Nina's. 'It is a—pleasure to meet you at last,' she murmured as she moved away, but her eyes said otherwise, and Nina's heart sank a little further. So, Louisa had been right, and she was not to be accepted by Anton's mother with any warmth.

'I have to go,' Anton cut into the tension filtering between the two women. 'Look after her for me, Mother,' he requested smoothly. 'Nina was just a little nervous of meeting you. Do your best to make her feel at home.'

Again, Nina picked up the hint of challenge in his voice, and knew for certain then that Anton had not had an easy time convincing his mother that Nina Lovell was the woman he wanted for his wife. Nina could understand it; she wasn't in the least bit convinced herself!

Nevertheless, she attempted to keep things on a polite footing. 'It—it was very good of you to come all this way to meet me, Mrs Lakitos,' she broke the stiff silence Anton left behind him.

'My son insisted on it.' Nina was bluntly informed. 'But I have to tell you, Miss Lovell, that Anton has grieved me bitterly with this shock decision.'

'I—I'm sorry.' The apology was genuine. She was sorry his mother was disappointed in her.

'You are not even Greek!'

Nina's smile was dry. 'No,' she confirmed. 'I am afraid I can't claim any Greek blood whatsoever.' But her chin came up in that brave way Ianthe's son would have recognised with wry dread. 'But my blood runs red, Mrs Lakitos,' she said, then added spiritedly, 'Just as I must assume yours does.'

'As red as your awful hair, no doubt.' The black eyes flicked contemptuously to Nina's silken halo of red-gold hair.

'I will not apologise for the colour of my hair.' Her hands were beginning to tremble, and she hid them into the folds of her gown. Anton had warned her not to spar with his mother, but it seemed he hadn't bothered warning his mother about the ground rules, because she was more than determined to provoke Nina!

'You are nothing but a child, and too slender for my taste!' The stiffly held mouth turned down in dislike. 'Will you apologise to me when that frail body of yours cannot produce the sons my son requires?'

'I am not marrying Anton for the exclusive function of giving him sons, Mrs Lakitos,' Nina answered stiffly, rising fully to the indignity of the inquisition.

'And why are you marrying him?' the Greek woman questioned coldly. 'For his money, is that it? Your own father's wealth is drying up, so you thought you would find yourself a nice rich husband?'

Nina laughed at that; she couldn't help it, it was so ridiculous. 'Why?' she threw back sweetly. 'Can't you believe your son capable of making a woman love him for himself alone?'

Ianthe stiffened with haughty affront. 'Anton can have any woman he likes!'

Nina nodded. 'Because his money draws them.' Too angry to care, she pressed home only what the woman herself had just implied. What was it with these Greeks that made them so condescendingly superior to everyone else?

'That is not what I meant at all!' his mother said irritably. 'You have to understand the ways of a Greek to understand what my son's announcement has done.' She went on coldly, 'Anton was expected to marry well. A Greek girl, one whose wealth and fortune would complement his own.'

Like the lovely Louisa for instance? Nina thought. She was well aware of the kind of money the Mandraki shipping family had behind them. 'My own father is not exactly penniless, you know,' she said defensively.

'We are talking pounds, not pennies, Miss Lovell,' Mrs Lakitos scorned. 'And we are talking blood. Good Greek blood which would reinforce the strength of our own pure Greek bloodline, not that weak stuff you were referring to a moment ago. You have to know what you are allowing him to throw away by agreeing to marry him.'

Nina was beginning to feel a bit like a Victorian maid, condemned for thinking she could marry a prince! 'So, what are you trying to suggest, Mrs Lakitos?' she enquired. 'That I jilt your son for his own good?'

'Ah.' Ianthe Lakitos smiled at last. 'I see you are beginning to understand.'

'That your son's happiness is up for sale like any commodity sold in the market-place?' she said. 'You're right, Mrs Lakitos, I am only just beginning to understand!'

'That is not what I meant!' Ianthe protested impatiently, actually looking uncomfortable at last. And Nina was angry enough to enjoy seeing it.

'You are still standing?' a deep voice remarked in surprise, and both women stiffened, glancing sharply around to find Anton just closing the drawing-room door. 'And no drinks!' he declared, seeming completely oblivious to the hostility permeating the air.

He strode forwards, smiling easily at both of them. 'I apologise for taking so long. It was a silly matter, but those are always the ones which seem to take up more of your time than they actually deserve. A sherry, Mother... ?'

It was an awful evening, and Nina had never been so glad to be helped into the back of the car as she was when Anton eventually brought the traumatic evening to an end.

'She hates me,' she said dully.

'Not hate,' he denied. 'Just—resentment of anyone who gets in the way of something she wanted very much.'

'The rich little Greek girl with the pedigree blood?' Nina jeered.

He had settled himself into the corner of the car as soon as they moved away, a mixture of jet lag and strain hollowing out the richly tanned lines of his face. 'Is that what she said?' His eyebrows rose in wry appreciation, mouth showing a humour which only served to make Nina more angry. 'She will come around eventually,' he assured her, closing his eyes. 'Just give her time.'

'If that is supposed to make me feel better, then let me disappoint you,' Nina snapped, 'I don't want her approval.' A full evening of having to endure his mother's only slightly less acid barbs while her son was present made her more than ready to pour all her frustrated anger over his thankless head. 'Or anyone else's for that matter.' Her angry eyes glinted at the darkness rushing by them outside the car. 'I am marrying you because we made a bargain, not with the ambition of becoming the light of your mother's life!'

'Or mine, for that matter.' The eyes remained closed, the voice flat.

'You want me, and you're going to get me,' she muttered. 'Don't expect more than that.'

'Oh, I shall expect a whole lot more than that, my spitting little kitten!' And with an economy of movement that set the nerves stinging across the surface of her skin he pulled her to him, sealing her mouth with kisses, turning her anger to passion without having to try very hard to do it. And at the same time forcing her to accept what any amount of words had failed to do: that even if she could escape the net being so ruthlessly thrown around her, she wouldn't want to.

She wanted this too much. Wanted him.

The private jet tilted as it hit an air pocket, and Nina stirred from the light doze she had fallen into. It had been a long and tiring journey, finishing off a long and tiring day.

They had been married that morning at a small church not far away from her home. She had worn traditional white satin and lace, and covered the strained pallor of her face with a full tulle veil. Her father had had tears in his eyes as he watched her come down the stairs. He was leaning heavily on the two sticks he was determined to discard once they reached the church. He still wasn't well, and Dr Martin had been concerned enough to insist he go straight back to bed once the traditional wedding toast had been drunk.

'Goodness, girl,' he muttered rustily, 'you look just like your mother.' And there were tears in his eyes as he bent to place a kiss on her cheek through the enveloping folds of tulle.

Anton's mother attended the ceremony, and her manner had not softened one iota since their first meeting. Louisa was there too, invited by Ianthe, who, Nina was sure, had done it solely to discomfit her, and she could feel the septic sting of Louisa's eyes on her back as she walked down the aisle to take Anton's waiting hand.

He looked devastating, dressed in a conventional dark suit and plain white shirt; nothing could take away the man's special charisma. His gaze narrowed on her face obscured by the veil, and she was glad of the cover, feeling the tiny muscles around her heart squeeze as she looked up at him.

His hand was warm and firm on her freezing cold one, long fingers closing around hers in a way which stated ownership.

Behind her followed a single bridesmaid, the only one from the music group who hadn't condemned her for jilting Jason. 'No contest,' Tina had announced after meeting Anton at the small dinner party her father had insisted on holding a few nights before the wedding. 'Want Jason after meeting him?' Her big eyes had rolled upwards expressively. 'It's like tasting caviare when you're only used to tuna fish. There is no comparison. You lucky devil, Nina.'

But Nina didn't feel lucky. She felt unbearably sad, and just a little afraid of what came after this very respectable ceremony. During the weeks leading up to the wedding, Anton had turned back into the remote stranger she had known while her father had lain seriously ill. He had visited her, been very polite, even quite gentle with her, but he hadn't kissed her once since that last passionate exchange in the rear of his chauffeur-driven car when he had pulled away from her, muttering, 'God, this has to stop, or you will be coming to me on our wedding night a very experienced woman!'

'What makes you think I'm not already experienced?' she'd flared, annoyed at his confidence in her innocence.

Black eyes had flashed darkly at her. 'You had better not be, Nina,' he'd warned, 'or you will find out just how Greek I am!'

'Is that why you wouldn't marry Louisa?' she had hit back tartly, certain as anything that it was Louisa whom his mother had picked out for his bride. 'Because you know she's no virgin?'

A dry smile had touched his mouth. 'You would have to go a long way back into Louisa's past to trace her virginity. No,' he'd then denied more seriously. 'I am not so primitive as to expect virginity from my wife on her wedding night—so long as it was I who took it from her in the first place.' He had cupped her cheek with a hand, holding her gaze with the black density in his. 'My Greek breeding demands total commitment from my wife, Nina. Remember that,' he'd advised. 'It will hold you in good stead if you ever consider cheating on me.'

'But I am not to demand the same of you, I suppose?'

'Before we met? No,' he'd said. 'The double standard raising its ugly head,' he had admitted drily. 'But since we met?' He'd pressed a final kiss to her lips before moving away from her. 'I give you leave to beat me to within an inch of my life if you ever catch me with another woman.'

'Catch being the operative word.'

He had just laughed, and settled himself back into his corner of the car to study her lazily while they finished their journey. Since then he had kept his distance, and the man she had become so reluctantly drawn towards had once again become the stranger she instinctively wanted to cower away from.

But his eyes were burning when he lifted the veil from her face. *Mine,* the look said, and she trembled when he bent to kiss her cold, stiff lips, as every fear she'd ever felt of him leapt starkly back to the surface.

'You will never keep him,' Louisa said confidently when she managed to corner Nina at the wedding breakfast. 'You just are not woman enough.'

'I shall learn to be,' she replied, refusing to let Louisa see how her words had struck home.

'I believe my son to have made the biggest mistake of his life today,' her new mother-in-law told her coldly. 'And I hold you entirely responsible for it all.'

Which probably held more truth than Ianthe actually realised, Nina acknowledged heavily to herself.

'Look after my girl,' her father gruffly commanded when at last he gave in to the doctor's urges to get him back to bed. 'And remember those grandsons you promised me!'

Her expression was troubled as she watched Dr Martin lead him away. 'Leave a sick old man his dreams,' Anton murmured quietly beside her, understanding the reason for her frown. 'Is it not the foremost hope of every parent when their offspring marry? Even my own mother has that broody glint in her eye,' he drawled, making Nina glance across the room to where Ianthe stood frowning at them. She wasn't brooding, Nina thought acidly. She was busy casting evil spells! 'What she loses on the swings, she hopes to gain on the roundabouts,' Anton mocked lightly.

'Which is why she continues to treat me like a leper.'

'Wait until the children come along,' he soothed, 'Then see how she responds to you.'

'What children?' she threw back tartly, aware of the odd clutching of her body at the thought of conceiving his child.

'The ones we will forge in a storm of fire and passion,' he promised, and she trembled at the deep growling promise in his voice. 'Frightened, Nina?' he taunted softly.

She went to deny it, then found she couldn't, lowering her eyes instead. 'I have to change,' she mumbled, desperate to get away from him, if only for a short while. And, thankfully, he let her go, but his soft laughter taunted her as she went...

'We are almost there,' a quiet voice said beside her, and Nina sat up straight, smothering a yawn as she turned to look out of the aeroplane window. 'The island is small, but large enough to accommodate a landing strip.'

'Does it have a name?' she asked, watching the baked brown oval shape of an island rise out of the Aegean sea. It was getting late, gone seven o'clock in the evening, and the August sun was polishing everything below them a rich copper colour.

'It is Lakitos Island, of course,' he said, sounding amused and not a little arrogant. 'It has been in the family for generations. The island is home to me—the only real home I ever really knew as a child because I used to spend all my holidays from school here.'

The wandering life of a diplomat's son, she recalled, feeling an odd sympathy for the boy who must have found his gypsy existence lonely sometimes.

'There is one small village—there...' he leaned across her to point down to where a cluster of flat-roofed white-washed buildings stood blushing in the evening sun. His arm pressed against her own, making it tingle, the musky male scent of him teasing her nostrils. 'It is a small island, dependent mainly on itself for its needs, and the boat that calls here once a fortnight during its round trip supplying all the smaller islands.'

'No tourists?' He was so close that she was hardly breathing, and desperately tried to keep her voice level.

He smiled—she sensed the movement of his mouth almost touching her cheek. 'We discourage tourism on this island. The tourists have more than enough of our homeland to assuage their hunger for sun-soaked mythology, and we have nothimg to offer them either in the way of history or accommodation. We are a simple people at heart, Nina,' he informed her drily. 'Give a Greek a modest home, a good wife, and a place he can congregate with his neighbours in the evening to drink *ouzo* and put the world to rights across a simple wooden table, and he will be content.'

At that moment, the plane banked sharply, throwing Anton hard against her, and he instinctively threw a hand across the front of her to hold her steady in her seat, brushing across the sensitive tips of her breasts as he did so. She sucked in a sharp breath, and he glanced at her, his eyes darkening as her soft mouth began to quiver.

'And th-the big house I can see on the hill-top?' she enquired breathlessly, knowing he wanted to kiss her, and praying to God that he wouldn't. She had a feeling she might shatter if he did, she felt so brittle.

He grimaced, easing the sexual pressure between them by sinking back into his own seat, arching a brow at her audible sigh of relief. 'Our villa,' he announced, then smiled ruefully. 'And not so modest, I suppose I had better add before you do.'

Nina stared down at the lovely sun-kissed villa with its two-storeyed verandas and whitewashed walls. She could see the rich blue rectangle of a swimming pool laid out in the middle of a mosaic patio, and the surprising lushness of lawn which swept down to a rock-rimmed beach.

'Water is not a problem on the island,' Anton said as though he only had to look at her to read her thoughts. 'It has its own natural spring which gives us more than enough not to have to worry about wasting it on keeping at least some of the land alive and fertile during the long hot summer.'

The plane lurched and landed on the ground with a bump, making Nina start in mild alarm. One moment they had been circling low over the island, the next landing without any warning whatsoever.

'Primitive but effective,' Anton drawled as the drag on the plane's brakes forced them back into their seats, pulling them to a stop almost as soon as they had all wheels on the ground.

He got up, smiling at her as he held out a hand to offer her assistance. She took it, dry-mouthed and tongue-tied. He was still wearing the same clothes he had worn to their wedding—minus the jacket and silk tie, and looking ten times more attractive without them. The white cotton shirt clung to the rigid walls of his chest, forming shadows where the thick mat of body hair curled in a dark disturbing triangle beneath. His hips were slim and spare, his stomach flat-planed so the dark trousers fitted snugly before following the powerful length of his legs.

He manoeuvred her in front of him, his hands possessive on her waist as he guided her down the aisle to where the steward was already unlocking the door. At the top of the steps, she paused, momentarily stunned by the bank of heat which hit her full in the face.

'All right?' Anton enquired from just behind her.

'Yes,' she whispered, her voice sounding rusty even to her own ears. 'I just didn't expect the heat to be so intense so late in the day, that's all.'

'Hmm.' His hands tightened a little on her waist. 'We must watch that delicate skin of yours does not burn, *agapi mou*. I couldn't bear to see its perfection marred by the ruthless heat of my Greek sun.'

'I shall be careful,' she promised, moving down the steps so that she could break free of him. He let her go, but only for as long as it took him to join her on the makeshift runway, then he was reaching for her shoulders and turning her around to face him.

'Welcome,' he said simply, and bent to capture her lips.

It wasn't a passionate kiss, or even a kiss that expected a response, but her breathing was unsteady when he drew away, and her cheeks had grown warmer, a bout of painful shyness completely overwhelming her.

'Let's go.' She heard the husky rumble of his voice and shivered delicately. Did she have any choice? she wondered sadly as she let him take her to where an open-topped Mercedes stood waiting for them not ten yards away, parked beneath the shade of a huge old olive tree. Any choices she might have had, she had let slip through her fingers weeks ago, she reminded herself heavily. For-feited on the night she had set out on her crazy mission of doom.

'Don't tremble so much,' he scolded as he walked beside her, his hand like a loose manacle around her own. 'I am not going to jump on you the moment we are alone.'

'I d-didn't think you were!' she denied, daring to send him an indignant glare.

'Liar,' was all he said, and she had to look quickly away from the lazy mockery in his deep brown eyes.

He saw her seated in the Mercedes before returning to the plane where the steward and the pilot were already taking off their luggage. The three men chatted genially for a few minutes, then shook hands, and Anton was picking up the two large suitcases and striding back to the car. He threw them on to the back seat, then climbed in beside her, his attention on acquiring his own comfort as he rolled back his shirt sleeves to the elbows and loosened several buttons on his shirt before reaching over to fire the car engine.

Nina had watched it all in a kind of hypnotic fasci-nation, but now she turned away from him as the sud-denly heady temptation to reach out and touch the newly exposed skin at his throat had her stomach knotting in appalled acknowledgement of her own hectic emotions. It was humiliating, the way her senses responded so vi-olently to him.

The dark sapphire on her finger glinted blue fire at her in the steadily dying sunlight, the addition of a heavily engraved wedding ring still feeling strange to her. She twisted the rings around absently, remembering how neat Jason's single diamond had looked on her slender hand, and a new sadness filled her heart.

Poor Jason, she had treated him so badly that she didn't think she would ever manage to justify it to her conscience. Yet, she admitted dully, even if she could have found a way to avoid committing herself so totally to the man beside her, she knew she wouldn't have used it. Anton had spoiled her chances of ever being content with any other man but him. He fired her senses in a way that exalted her even as it appalled. One kiss was all it took, one small, insignificant kiss like the one he had laid on her lips as they left the plane just now, and he could turn her into a shaking mass of emotion.

She heard the revving of the plane engines as Anton turned the car on to a dusty track and began accelerating away. The speed pushed the warm air through her loose hair, and she lifted her face to it, staring up at the rich expanse of deep blue sky above.

So, this is it, she told herself bleakly. This was what she had committed herself to. A husband she knew she would never be sure of, and the unnerving prospect of a wedding night she knew was going to alter the whole substance of her life.

'There will be a small reception committee when we arrive, I'm afraid.' Anton's rueful tone broke into her bleak thoughts. 'People from the village,' he explained. 'It is customary for them to welcome you as my wife.'

She turned to look at him. His black hair was blowing in the breeze, his beautifully honed face looking more arrogant, more handsome than she had ever seen it, with the warm caress of his own Greek sun highlighting the richness of his skin.

He caught her staring at him, and a rakish grin cut a dashing line across his features. 'Do you think you will be able to handle it?' he challenged lazily.

'I don't know.' She looked away from him. 'Do you think I will?'

'Oh, I think so,' he drawled. They were driving up a gently winding incline, the view blocked off on either side by tall stately fir trees. 'You will probably send them that shy little smile of yours which holds a certain charm along with the reserve, and they will be bewitched, just as I was when I first encountered it. And if that does not work . . .' he continued while she gasped, stopping the car with a jerk then turning fully to face her, his gaze running over the tumble of fiery hair ' . . . then that lovely hair will. They will think I've brought my own personal goddess to the island, and, before you know it, they will be erecting shrines to you!'

'Shrines are for saints!' she snapped, disturbed by his light-hearted flippancy, for it held a hint of pride which moved her oddly. 'And God knows,' she sighed, 'I am no saint.' Saints didn't seethe with lust every time they look at a man.

There was a small silence, when Nina found she couldn't look at him and Anton sat beside her studying her pale tense profile for so long that she thought she would have to start screaming just to ease the tension around them.

'W-why have we stopped?' she asked instead, glancing around and seeing nothing that even vaguely resembled the lovely white house she had seen from the air.

'Come on.' He got out of the car, obviously expecting her to do the same, which she did, and they met at the car bonnet. Anton took her hand in his and began drawing her between two fir trees, then stopped, bringing her to stand in front of him.

'Look,' he said. 'I thought it might give you pleasure to see this. We could not have picked a better moment to be driving by this particular spot.'

'Oh——!' she gasped in pleasant surprise, focusing on the beautiful spread of Aegean sea basking in the glory of a red fire sunset. Everything around them seemed to be blushing, from the semicircular curve of sun-bleached rock that formed the sides of a tiny bay, to the soft golden circle of sand on the beach below. Deep purple shadows stood out as if etched in by an artist's pen, and out at sea the large ball of fire seemed to be performing a careful balancing trick on the very edge of the horizon.

'Apollo,' Anton chanted softly, his arm closing around her waist to gently urge her back against him, 'the sun god, joins Zeus in the heavens with Poseidon in the sea. It is an awesome meeting, is it not?'

She nodded, her body unconsciously leaning into his as they continued to watch as the sun slowly sunk into the sea, the scene in front of them changing fascinatingly as it did so.

Then it wasn't the heavenly view in front of her which held her attention, but the man standing so close behind, as his hand began tracing a light caress along the smooth flesh of her uncovered arm until it reached the feathery ends of her hair, and began absently fondling the silken strands, making her scalp tingle pleasurably and her heart beat faster.

'Beautiful,' he murmured huskily.

'Yes,' she whispered, turning her head so she could smile at him. 'It's...' She got no further, the words dying in her throat when she saw the darkened heat of his gaze. He was looking at her, not at the sunset, his tanned face burnished by the quickly fading sun.

'You are beautiful, Nina,' he murmured again, and lowered his mouth on to hers.

She thought of protesting, even stiffened a little in his arms with the beginnings of rejection, but something in the magic of the moment had her mouth parting beneath his, and she allowed him to turn her fully in his arms, her body arching sensuously into the kiss.

'Nina...' he sighed against her lips. Then the world seemed to stand still, life beginning and ending with this poignant moment. And her mouth blossomed for him, their tongues touching on an electrifying meeting of the senses.

It was the most intimate kiss they had ever exchanged, overshadowing anything that had gone before it, and she found herself held by it, her hands drifting along the rigid muscles of his arms until they wound around his neck, her body stretching and bending with such innate sensuality that he shuddered as he held her.

By the time they broke apart, the darkness had fallen all around them. Nina swayed dizzily, disorientated by the kiss, by the inspiring sunset, and by the man who held her so possessively to him.

'Let's go home,' he said, and Nina trembled, knowing with a fresh surge of trepidation just what that meant.

CHAPTER EIGHT

NEITHER Anton nor Nina spoke as they drove the few hundred extra yards to the villa; neither seemed capable. Nina could sense the dark tension in him as he drove, felt the exact same thing in herself, and sat very still beside him, not knowing what to do to ease the terrible pressure and afraid of what would happen once he decided to.

They turned a bend in the road, the car headlights swinging in a wide arc across the night sky, filling her with an alarming awareness of their isolation. Then the villa was there, the white walls illuminated by the car's lights, mingling with the added warmth of light spilling golden and welcoming from the villa windows.

At least half a dozen people were waiting at the top of the veranda steps. Nina felt the tug of apprehension for this next ordeal in a long line of ordeals, and made a firm effort to get a control on her nerves before anyone noticed.

He brought the car to a stop at the bottom of the steps, ignoring all the expectant faces as he murmured, 'Stay there,' to her and got out of the car, coming around to her side to open the door himself then bending to take her arm.

She hadn't done a good job at calming her nerves, she realised when he bent his head to urge softly, 'Be brave—this will only take a moment, then we will be left alone.'

Was that supposed to make her feel better? She wasn't sure which alarmed her more—the prospect of meeting all those dark, beaming faces he was guiding her towards, or all that aloneness he had so casually referred to!

He began speaking in Greek, his smile rueful, the arm he had around her possessive as he led her up the steps and to an over-large lady dressed all in black, her round face smiling warmly.

'Agnes,' he informed Nina. 'Our housekeeper and the woman who tanned my backside more times than I care to remember when I was a child on this island.'

Nina sent Agnes a shy smile, then found herself enveloped in a smothering bear-hug of an embrace, the flourish of Greek spoken to her sailing right over the top of her self-conscious head.

Then Leon, Giorgio, Athene...her mind began to boggle as she was passed from one person to another, all smiling a warm welcome, all holding some important post on the small island, though the significance of them was way beyond her powers of comprehension. Anton was smiled at, teased, slapped on the back by the men and embraced by the women. Her shy blushes were ignored as she was remarked over, dissected in detail then put back together again, and, in general, made to feel more welcome by these strangers than she had ever been made to feel in her life.

Then Anton was sending out some rueful command that had everyone laughing as they made their mass exodus from the veranda—except for Agnes who had obviously decided to take charge of Nina, her plump hand firm on her arm, her tongue clicking in a Greek version of motherly attention in between rapping out stern commands to Anton who, to Nina's surprise, obeyed without a single protest.

She was led into the coolness of a hallway, the cream-painted walls and honey-coloured tiled floor all seeming to endorse the warmth of her welcome here.

'See—see...' Agnes kept saying eagerly, taking Nina up the stairs and along a spacious landing to a raw-grained light wood door which she threw open then stood back to allow Nina to precede her inside. 'See...!' she exclaimed again, using the only English word she seemed to know, and waddled past Nina to go over to the bed, pressing energetically down on the mattress, white teeth shining as merrily as her eyes. 'See...'

'What she is trying to say...' drawled a lazily amused voice that made Nina spin around to find Anton standing there with their suitcases '... is that this is our bedroom. She is not...' he then added drily as he swung into the room '... trying to order us straight into the marriage bed!'

Had her terrified expression told him that much? She blushed, looking away from both dark faces which were grinning like alien monsters to her agitated mind.

The room was, she found when her eyes managed to focus on her surroundings, quite nice, the simplistic taste of the wealthy Greek having an underplayed luxury about it that pleased the eye. The walls were cream-painted again, on bare plaster, the furniture, like the doors, a pale wood, hand-carved and tailor built to fit the room. Island made, she guessed, with love and pride worked into every detail. The most beautiful handmade lace curtains hung across the open window, billowing gently in the evening breeze, and the same snowy lace covered the bed—a huge bed—a bed she absolutely refused to look at while those two pairs of eyes were watching her so intently.

The sound of cases being dropped on the floor made her start nervously. 'The bathroom is through that door.' Anton pointed, ignoring her nervous reaction. He ignored the second one too when his hands came warmly on her shoulders. 'Say "thank you" nicely to Agnes.' The mockery in his voice made her blushes darken. 'Then we will leave you alone to—get your bearings.'

She turned shyly to face the waiting housekeeper whose round face was looking expectantly at her. 'How do I say it in Greek?' she asked the man standing close behind her.

For some reason, the enquiry affected him, because he didn't answer right away, his thumbs tracing gentle circles on the tensed muscles at her nape. 'You are a thoughtful child, Nina Lakitos,' he murmured eventually, and the simple sound of her new name on his lips made her quiver a little desperately inside. 'Say "*efkharisto*, Agnes," and she will be your slave for life.'

Sending Agnes a nervous little smile, she repeated what Anton had instructed her to say. Sure enough, the housekeeper's face became wreathed in smiles, a bewildering flow of Greek coming right back at her which made her blink and Anton grin. 'She wants me to tell you that she thinks I am the luckiest man on earth to find such a lovely wife.'

Nina began to wonder if her cheeks would ever be allowed to cool down as once again she felt the betraying blush creep along them. 'Th-thank you.' she said shyly. '*Efkharisto*, Agnes,' she repeated, receiving yet another stream of bewildering Greek in return.

Anton laughed, and made some amused reply. 'Agnes says she will spare your blushes and see us both in the morning,' he translated as Agnes nodded, beamed, and bowed herself out of the room.

Which left only him.

She was so uptight that her nerve-ends felt stretched to breaking point. She couldn't look at him, and a tense silence inched its way around them. After a moment, he sighed softly and moved away, walking back to the door while she bit down hard on her bottom lip, waiting for him to leave her alone as he had promised to do.

So when he didn't leave, but closed the door instead, she almost wept. 'No, Anton, please...' She was already backing away from him although he hadn't moved from the door.

' "No, Anton, please"—what?' he taunted huskily.

His eyes were filled with lazy heat. He looked like a man with a brand new possession, excited, eager to learn all about it, and she swallowed tensely.

'D-don't tease me,' she whispered, lowering her hot face from his gaze. 'Y-you said you would give me time alone to—to get my...'

'Bearings,' he finished for her. 'Yes, I did say that, didn't I?' He sounded as though he was regretting that moment of charity now. 'A kiss.' He decided. 'One small kiss, then I will leave you alone, Nina, and that is a promise.'

The husky quality in his voice alone made her tremble, the hungry gleam in his eyes drying her mouth until she had to moisten her lips with the nervous flick of her tongue. She shook her head, the long flow of red-gold hair like a halo of fire around the creamy perfection of her face.

'Come here,' he commanded gruffly.

Her stomach turned over and she shook her head again, 'Please...' she pleaded unsteadily, her blue eyes much too big in her pale young face.

'Now.'

Not daring to take him on in this mood, she moved forwards on shaky legs to come to a nervous standstill in front of him.

'So shy.' His hand came out to curve the side of her jaw. 'So utterly sweet and innocent. It almost seems a shame to take it all from you.' His wide chest lifted and fell on a despairing sigh. 'But take it I will,' he vowed. 'With fire and passion and a devastating sensuality. I'll change the child into woman, then worry myself to grey hair at the Pandora's box I will have opened!'

'I'm not like that,' she denied, inhaling sharply as his hand came up to boldly cup her breast in an outright gesture of ownership. The firm young peak beneath his palm stung as it swelled in response.

'No?' he mocked her denial. 'You are too inexperienced to know what kind of woman you are going to be. A child, Nina,' he muttered thickly, all signs of gentle indulgence gone as he suddenly pulled her against him.

'You are a child, who has no idea of the power her womanhood will have over mere mortal men!'

'No——!' Frightened by the words, by the hot passion he threaded into each one of them, she tried to pull away.

'And mine!' he growled, refusing to let her go. 'Mine, to have and possess—and know as no other man will ever know!'

Ever since the kiss in the sunset, he had been vibrating with a need she feared was bordering on the uncontrolled, and now that fear was confirmed as his hand tightened on her breast, crushing the breath from her lungs as a thousand needles of hot, sharp pleasure scattered through her. He muttered something beneath his breath, then his mouth came on to hers with an ardour that bordered on the angry, and she melted, hating herself for it, but unable to stop the degeneration of everything sensible inside her. He was like a drug in her system; she hated everything about it, but couldn't get enough of it, and the more she got, the more she wanted.

She was a trembling mass of emotion by the time he dragged his mouth from hers. She kept her lashes lowered so he couldn't see the agony of confusion rioting inside her. Her kiss-swollen lips were hot and quivering, and she wanted desperately to lift her fingers to them, feel the changes he had effected on them, knowing that, like her breast, her mouth had blossomed for him, and hating that weakness also.

'Be at ease,' he muttered, thrusting her away with hands which weren't quite steady, his dark face flushed as he turned abruptly away. 'I am not so savage that I would rip your virginity from you on the first moment we have been left alone.' Then he left the room with a controlled violence that displayed the battle going on inside him.

Nina sank down weakly on the bed. He wanted her so badly that there seemed little chance of him managing to be gentle with her. He had to know that as well as she did, which was, perhaps, why he had uttered that final supposedly comforting statement.

And suddenly the full magnitude of what she had let herself in for by marrying him almost had her jumping up and running, screaming from the room.

But there was no escape. Not from him or his island. She was committed, trapped in every way a woman could be. Married to a man whose desires terrified her even as her own leapt up to greet them. Married to a man who didn't love her, though, again, she had an awful feeling that she could just have been foolish enough to fall in love with him. And married to a man who could, at any moment, tire of her, walk away and leave her, and in so doing shatter everything she had left within.

Getting up, she wandered over to the lace-curtained window and lifted the fine fabric aside to step out on to the veranda. The air was cooler now, though still warm to her unaccustomed skin. She sighed softly, moving to lean against the white-painted balustrade, looking up at the velvet-dark sky above, with its celebration of twinkling lights. It was a beautiful night, the silence broken only by the intermittent call of the cicadas hidden in the sweet-smelling shrubbery below. Her fingers picked lightly at her folded arms, the action unconsciously comforting.

She was here, the wife of a man whose blood ran as hot and free as the sun that drenched his island with its scorching heat each day. Up there, beyond the curtain of glittering stars, played his gods, the mythical conquerors of life itself.

Were they watching her now, she wondered fancifully, waiting curiously to see how the little English girl coped with one of their blessed descendants?

She smiled, a half-wry, half-bitter smile, and turned back to the bedroom. She knew how she would cope. Anton would consume her, devour her with his passion, and she wanted him to.

That just about said it all, she accepted heavily as she went in search of the bathroom.

She found Anton in a pleasantly old-fashioned kitchen when she went looking for him, seated at a scrubbed kitchen table with a cup of strong Greek coffee at his elbow and a Greek newspaper spread out in front of him. He glanced up and smiled as she entered, but other than that showed no hint of that barely leashed hunger she had witnessed earlier.

'There is coffee if you want it,' he murmured casually, returning his attention to his paper.

'I—anything cold?' she asked, shifting nervously from one foot to the other.

Lowered eyes observed her hoodedly, but didn't look up. 'Of course. In the fridge.' A hand made a lazy wave across the kitchen. 'Help yourself,' he invited.

She found a jug of freshly squeezed orange juice, the smooth glass chill to the touch. Her mouth watered as she took it out of the fridge and went in search of a glass, pouring herself a generous amount and gulping at it thirstily.

He flipped over a sheet of newspaper, and she found her gaze drawn to the contrast between the white paper and his long brown fingers. Something moved inside her, an awakening of the senses again, and she held her breath for a long high-pressured moment to contain the feeling, then exhaled slowly, and made a concerted effort to behave like an adult rather than a fool, moving with the jug and glass to sit down opposite him.

'Everything looks very—prepared,' she observed.

Black eyes flicked towards her then away again. 'Agnes would be appalled if you had said otherwise.'

She lifted the jug and poured herself another glass of orange. 'Would she normally live in here if we weren't— we weren't . . . ?' God, this was awful! She couldn't even speak without . . .

'Agnes has her own house just a ten-minute walk away,' he put in smoothly, taking a sip at his coffee, reading his paper.

Nina ran her fingertips down the ice-cool glass where the condensation had already hidden the contents from view. He really was the most attractive man she had ever seen. She couldn't seem to keep her eyes off him, was fascinated by every nuance of the man. Like his hair, so black and sleek, expensively styled and cut to suit his well-shaped head. His lashes were long and thick, lying in two perfect arcs against his high cheekbones. His dark brown eyes so...

'But she cares for this place as if it were her own...'

...Brown eyes so warm and seductive, except when he was angry, then they turned into black voids, hard and chilling. His nose was long and slender, not quite Roman, not quite Greek. His mouth was wide and naturally sensual, his chin square, a rock, like the man, a rock a woman could maroon herself on if she had the courage.

Another sheet of paper flicked over, and she started, blinking as she caught his sudden glance in her direction from beneath those beautiful dark lashes, and she quickly dropped her gaze. The tension inside her inched up a few more notches. She wasn't going to be able to carry this thing through, she thought desperately. He looked so different here, in his natural surroundings, dark and...

'Agnes prides herself on always being prepared for my arrival with or without prior warning...'

...And alien. That worldly sophistication transforming itself into something far more...

'Though I usually like to give her fair warning. It is only courteous...'

...Intimidating. She lifted her eyes to him again, finding them drawn to the deep triangle of warm skin exposed at his chest where the white shirt had been tugged open to low down on the taut planes of his stomach. The dark hair was thick and crisp, a curling mass of masculinity, the breastplate beneath firmly muscled, the brown skin sheened like stretched silk over...

'Nina...'

She jumped violently, almost spilling the glass as her eyes jerked upwards to clash with his.

He looked grim, the paper lowered to the table, long fingers clenched tightly on the flimsy sheets.

'If you don't stop it,' he warned her quietly, 'you will find yourself in a whole lot of trouble...'

His mouth had a fascinating shape to it when he spoke, it seemed to form words with a...

A hot flush mounted her skin, beginning at the agitated rise and fall of her breasts and running along her throat and across her cheeks. 'I...' She licked her dry lips. He looked tense, angry almost. 'I was miles away,' she lied. 'W-what did you say?'

'I said,' he murmured silkily, holding her still with the fixed darkness of his gaze, 'I said, be careful or you may find yourself...'

She got up, the chair scraping across the tiled floor and making her cringe inside. 'Is it all right if I go for a walk outside?' she asked jerkily, sounding like a child asking permission from an adult, and she groaned inside at the mess she was making of all this. He had been speaking to her in a studiedly calm and easy flow, as if he knew what was going on inside her and was trying to gentle her out of her fears. But even his voice sounded different here, the depth more liquid, the accent more seductive. She could barely breathe through the sexual tension she was experiencing, and what made it all worse was that she knew just who was generating it, and it wasn't the man sitting watching her!

'You can do whatever you want to do here, Nina,' he said softly. 'So long as you don't try running away.'

It was that obvious? 'I—I'm sorry,' she stammered again. 'It—it's just that I...'

'That you are so uptight about what happens next that you can hardly think of anything else!' he bit out angrily. 'For God's sake!' he sighed. 'calm down! I have already assured you that I am not going to jump on you. I'm not that desperate.'

But he was! She was! Oh, God, what was happening to her? She moved warily backwards, her wide blue gaze never shifting from his darkly frowning face.

Anton muttered a soft curse beneath his breath. 'Come on, then,' he said impatiently, getting to his feet. 'We'll go for a walk outside. Maybe that will help you to relax a little. Then I will——'

'No—please!' The very thought of his coming any- where near her turned her limbs to jelly. There was a terrible battle of wills going on inside her. She only had to look at him to want him shamefully, yet the very thought of him touching her made her quake with fear.

He was standing tall and grim now, watching her through the brooding curve of his lashes, and she lifted pleading eyes to his, not knowing what she was begging for except maybe her sanity, for she had a feeling she was losing it rapidly.

He continued to study her for a few moments longer, taking in the way she trembled, the whiteness of her strained face, the shocking battle going on behind the turbulent blue of her eyes, then he sighed heavily.

'What's the use?' she heard him mutter, shaking his dark head as he began walking towards her, and Nina whimpered at what she saw written in his eyes, horrified by her own behaviour, frightened by his. 'We may as well get it over with,' he said grimly. 'Then maybe you will stop jumping like a terrified kitten every time I so much as glance at you!'

'No, Anton, I...' Her hand went out in trembling appeal in front of her, she backing off as he came re- lentlessly forward. He caught the hand and pulled her determinedly against him.

'God, just look at you,' he growled, the impatience tinged with a pity that made her want to weep. 'Why does the idea of becoming one with me seem such a terrible thing?'

'I'm tired, Anton,' she pleaded in her own defence, the wild flurry of awareness already attacking her with just the simple act of his touch. Her frantic gaze caught his again, and her mouth began to tremble uncontrollably. 'Please,' she appealed. 'Let me go—just for tonight, let me sleep alone so I can——'

'No.' It was an intractable refusal. 'Putting off the inevitable will not make the horror any easier to face tomorrow—or the next day, or even the next if you were thinking you could hold me off that long.' A wry smile twisted his fascinating mouth. 'You are my wife now, Nina,' he reminded her. 'And tonight you are going to be treated as such.' And with a determined tug he pulled her against him. 'You've showered,' he murmured as he bent his face to her clean-scented throat, his fingers burrowing into her hair so he could tilt her head back for his seeking mouth. 'You smell of roses and maidenly innocence.'

'Please...' she cried, straining away from his searching mouth.

'Too late, my poor confused darling,' he whispered, 'You should not have admired me with your eyes just now. I am man enough to be aroused by such blatant invitation.'

His mouth came warmly on her own, easily parting her lips to accept the moist caress of his tongue and, scooping her into his arms, he began walking, moulding her to him as he strode out of the kitchen and up the stairs, the kiss holding her captive as he walked into the bedroom and over to where the huge bed waited expectantly for them.

Lowering her feet to the floor, he lifted his mouth only long enough to study the effect of his kiss in her dark, slumberous eyes, then he was kissing her again, no rush, no urgency any more, but with a slow deepening of sensuality which held her still and compliant in his arms.

He undressed her slowly, the slight tremor in his fingers making her breath leave her lungs in soft, agitated gasps. Discarded pieces of clothing were replaced by the tantalising caress of his lips. Nina squeezed her eyes shut and prayed she would get through this without dying. She felt as though she were dying; every sense in her was fluttering in desperate need to escape from the rigid control she was holding over them.

She flinched when his hand came to cover her breast, the stinging contact forcing her eyes wide to clash with the dark intensity of his. She was standing naked in front of him, the gentle breeze drifting in through the window disturbing the fine threads of her hair as he stepped back a little to look at her, black eyes hot and dense.

'The lights, Anton,' she pleaded huskily. 'Put out the lights.'

'No,' he refused. 'The last time you came to my bed, it was in darkness. This time we will finish what began there in the full glory of fire and light!'

He scooped her up again, lying her on the bed and bending over her to press a hard kiss to her lips before straightening away to remove his own clothes. Nina closed her eyes, and heard his soft, mocking laugh taunt her shyness.

He was already breathing disjointedly when he joined her on the bed, his arms reaching for her with an eagerness which fired the need in her own blood and had her moving to him without protest, curling into the shocking beauty of his body with such unconscious sensuality that he shuddered.

'My God, Nina,' he whispered hoarsely. 'You want this as much as I do!'

She didn't deny it, couldn't. He was right, and she did want him, with a fire that easily matched his own.

And every prediction he had made about their coming together came to fruition that long, hot, turbulent night, as he opened up the Pandora's box of her desires and let them fly wild and free.

It was awful, it was shocking, it was shamefully exhilarating. And the sheer intensity of it sent her soaring to incredible heights. She opened her eyes to see the shock mingling with the rapture on his passion-locked face, and knew it had stunned him too.

Her arms snaked up around his neck, pulling him down on to her, some terrible she-devil inside her exulting in the power she had discovered over this man.

He shuddered, his mouth opening on her breast, 'Nina...' he whispered thickly. 'God, Nina...'

In the grim grey cast of the early dawn, when at last he had fallen into an exhausted sleep, she lay looking at the shocked pallor of his face, and tears filled her tired eyes, tears of shame and horror and a certain hopelessness.

Months ago, when those black eyes had first looked at her and announced their desire, she had instinctively backed away. Weeks ago, in the confusing aggression of her own folly, she had been forced to recognise why. Now, in the grey half-light of a brand new day, she knew it all, and the tears brimmed and fell, tracing lazy channels down her pale cheeks. She loved this man, loved him with every fibre of her being, and there wasn't a single thing she could do about it.

The tears dried as she lay there, and slowly her own eyes grew heavy, closing out the sight and sounds echoing in her mind, the aching replay of her own total capitulation, and her only saving grace in it all had been that small cry she had made as he entered her.

'I hate you, Anton,' she'd whispered threadily as the fire threatened to consume her forever.

'No, you don't,' he'd muttered, his voice nothing but an ebbing wave rasping over her desire. 'You only wish you did.'

He was right, as he had been so right about everything from the very beginning. She didn't hate, she loved. And as sleep dragged her slowly into its darkened pits, her hand slipped lightly across his chest to curve into the warm moist nape of his neck, and she sighed, with no idea that the black eyes flicked open at the first whispering touch of her hand, and that the man beside her took over the sleepless vigil for a while, watching her as she slept, his thoughts as bleak and brooding as her own had been.

They slept on into the fierce heat of the morning, waking with their bodies curved together and the rattling sounds of cups on a tray to tell them they were no longer alone. Nina pushed her blushing face into his shoulder as Agnes chatted out a stream of Greek to the wry faced man holding his new wife so closely to him.

'She's gone,' he said teasingly when at last the silence came back to the sunny room.

Nina couldn't look at him, the drama of the night before holding her trapped in an all-consuming shyness. His hand touched her cheek, drawing a soft caress down to the point where her small chin curved delicately into her throat, and, with a gentle pressure, he urged her face up to his.

'All right?' he questioned gravely.

His eyes were dark and sombre, the genuine concern in them warming her. 'Yes,' she breathed, unable to manage more than that before her lashes were letting her hide again.

'I didn't—hurt you?'

She shook her head. No, there had been no pain, or none she could remember. Only the wild, white-hot need to feel him inside her, and the short, sharp stab of that union, welcomed by her overwrought senses.

'But I shocked you,' he said, not a question but a statement of grim fact.

She had shocked herself. The depth of his passions had always been clear. Her own had shocked both of them.

'I'm sorry,' he was saying, his hand drawing an absent caress down the side of her body where it curved intimately into his own. 'I lost control. The waiting had been such utter hell...'

Yes, she could accept that, understanding as she now did. The terrible build-up of sexual tension over the weeks had brought about the violent explosion, on both sides.

She trembled as his hand found her breast and cupped it gently, and she lifted disturbed eyes to his, the need inside her flaring in a way that held her trapped, and caught at his breath as he observed it.

'Hell, Nina...' He moved to lean over her, eyes dark and troubled even as his own need leapt to meet with hers. 'You terrify me,' he groaned, and covered her waiting mouth with his own.

CHAPTER NINE

IT SET the pattern for their whole stay. Nina and Anton were supposed to spend a fortnight on the island, but stayed a month, and during that time found a certain kind of peace with each other that Nina instinctively knew would not survive the return to reality.

Perhaps he knew it too, which was why he decided to stay on, though he was forced to spend some time in his study, dealing with business via the telephone and the complicated-looking computer system he had installed in there.

But by tacit agreement neither of them mentioned subjects liable to bring a return of the resentments they had managed to set aside. The woven threads of this new relationship were just too thin to take any pressure from outside sources, and the hostility which had brought them together in the first place was still there, lurking in the background, biding its time, holding a part of her back from him that she knew annoyed him.

But to commit her whole self totally to this man would be foolish, although she almost succumbed to the need to do just that the morning after their night of frenzied loving, when he led her into the sunny sitting-room at the villa and said huskily, 'I was going to buy you diamonds, but I remembered you voicing a dislike for jewellery and thought maybe you would get more pleasure out of this.'

This was a beautiful creamy white grand piano, standing in a shaded corner of the room. And Nina felt her heart fill with emotion.

'Oh, Anton...' she quavered, too moved to say anything more.

'I have had one installed in every home we have,' he informed her, that possessive 'we' sending warm tingles up and down her spine. 'I may have taken away your studies, Nina, but I had no wish to take away your music.'

'Thank you.' Her eyes were shining with happy tears when she turned to throw her arms around his neck in her very first unreserved move towards him.

And that precious moment was the closest she ever came to telling him how deeply she loved him, especially when his arms came tightly around her, and he murmured fiercely, 'I want you to be happy with me, *agapi mou*,' as though it meant more to him than anything else in the world.

But then, as she lifted her face to offer those fateful words which would commit her to him forever, she saw that the dark gleam was back in his eyes, and, on a lusty growl, he picked her up and took her back to bed. And any thought of using words of love to him died at that moment. His own feelings were all too clear.

Physical, nothing more, nothing less.

He wanted her, all the time, any time, and the desire didn't show any signs of abating as the days went by, more the opposite, his Greek nature making him jealously possessive of every smile, every moment of her time, until she began teasing him about it.

Then the day came when everything came to a head, as, she supposed later, it had to do when a man like Anton Lakitos found himself stuck with a woman who had suddenly realised the power of her own sexuality, and was taunting him ruthlessly with it, heady, almost drunk on the little victories she could win over him with just a look, or a certain provoking word. It was a sop to her own aching heart, she knew that, but couldn't stop herself from behaving like a siren when it provoked such exciting results.

He caught her talking to the fishermen down by the village one morning. She had left him at the villa working in his study, her usual routine of spending her time alone sitting at the piano, broken by a sudden urge to walk barefooted along the water's edge until she found herself by the village where several small fishing boats were just putting in after a long night out at sea.

It must have been the lack of piano music drifting around him as he worked which alerted him to this change in her routine, and Anton came looking for her, his face like thunder when he found her, wearing nothing more modest than one of his own white linen shirts over a skimpy white bikini, her wild hair in a glorious tumble down her back as she stood there laughing delightedly at the silly hand signals she was having to use to make herself understood, the fishermen grinning white-toothed with amusement as they struggled with their own pidgin English replies.

'You are not safe to be let near any man!' Anton growled as he dragged her away with the fishermen's teasing laughter ringing in their ears.

'Why not?' she challenged, thrilling inside at his jealous rage. 'Do you think I'm going to tear off their clothes if you let me escape long enough?'

'I will never give you the chance to try!'

'Then God help you when we get back to civilisation,' she drawled, pulling provokingly against the hard clasp of his hand as he launched them both back up the incline from the village to the villa. 'Unless, of course, you're planning to shut me away in a darkened room, and only let me out for your own pleasure.'

'I may never let you leave this island!' he threatened, stopping so he could glare down the long length of his nose at her in what she had come to recognise as his haughty look—he only did it when he wanted to intimidate.

'But that would mean leaving me alone with all those hot-blooded fishermen,' she reminded him silkily, and watched fascinated as dark colour streaked across his cheek bones.

'I'll kill you if you so much as look at another man! Got that?'

'Yes, sir!' she snapped to a mocking attention, looking so utterly wild and wanton with her hair flowing all around her taunting face that he yanked her to him, his mouth covering hers with a kiss meant to punish rather than please.

In equal aggression, she kissed him back, absorbing the punishing thrust of his tongue with the sensual flick of her own. Battles, they battled on every level. Where she got it from, Nina had no idea, but there was an inner devil inside her that made her want to match him whatever he did to her, though she had an awful feeling it was born out of fear, the fear that if she didn't keep his interest alive, then his passion would die along with it, and then she would have nothing left to hold him with.

His arms gripped her shoulders to push her at arm's length from him, black eyes boring into defiant blue. 'I'll get the better of you yet, you provocative little witch!' he scowled, and dragged her back to the villa to make love to her until she begged for mercy.

And when she lay, nothing but a boneless mass of aching compliance in his arms, he got up and left her, walking out of the room to leave her cold and trembling, shaking with frustration, and appalled at how easily he had been able to turn his own desire aside, his point well and truly made.

He locked himself in his study and she didn't see him for the rest of the day. And she punished him by going nowhere near the piano and let the silence filling the villa speak for itself, though neither did she venture outside. By the time they sat down to dinner, the tension between them was about as bad as it had ever been. Nina was riding her high horse of indignity, and he had withdrawn behind a cold shell of arrogance she knew she couldn't penetrate, even if she wanted to, which she didn't, she told herself mulishly as she dragged herself off to bed that night.

For the first time in a month, she had the bed to herself.

The next morning the telephone call came, ruining with a single shattering blow any hope of their resolving this first real dissension between them.

She was sitting drinking Agnes's freshly squeezed orange juice on the sunny patio when he came looking for her. And she was alerted the moment he sat down beside her and took her hands in his.

'Nina...' he began quietly.

'What's happened?' she gasped, eyes already wide with fear as they leapt up to meet the dark gravity in his.

'It's your father,' he said very gently. 'He's had another heart attack.'

They travelled back by private jet, Anton quietly supportive, wisely allowing her to sink into herself to wait out the long journey home.

Jonas wasn't dead, but very ill.

They arrived at the house in the cool dusk of an early September evening, Nina shivering a little at the drastic change in the temperature from Greece to England. She left Anton's side the moment they entered the house, going straight upstairs and into her father's bedroom to almost faint at the sight of his grey, sunken face.

Anton followed at a slower pace, to find her kneeling by her father's bed in much the same way he had seen her once before, his limp hand clutched tightly between hers. After a while, he moved away, drawing up the big easy chair and silently urging her into it. She didn't acknowledge him, and he left her, coming back hours later with the nurse the doctor had employed when Jonas took ill; stubbornly removing Nina from the room and down the stairs, he forced her to eat something

'I can't leave him,' she said flatly.

'Did I say I expected you to?' Dark brows lifted in faint affront at her inference. 'Of course your place is here while Jonas is so ill.'

Relief took some of the strain from her face, a face which had lost most of the lovely golden bloom it had acquired on the island.

'I shall stay here with you, of course,' he went on decidedly. 'It will prove no hardship to move my business operations into your father's study and——'

'No!' Her slender body stiffened out of the chair, the lingering shock and the awful worry bruising the soft skin around her eyes. 'I—you—I can't sleep with you here!' she cried, covering her face with a trembling hand at his look of pained surprise at her unexpected outburst. 'You have to understand,' she pleaded thickly, shuddering at the very idea of lying boneless in his arms while her father lay so ill. 'I can't be that person I was on the island. I j-just can't...'

His arms, coming warmly around her, cut off her broken attempt to explain. 'It's all right,' he said quietly. 'I do understand.'

'I'm so sorry,' she whispered, allowing herself the luxury of leaning against the solid support of his body. 'I know this w-wasn't part of our bargain, but——'

'What are you talking about?' he cut in gruffly, thrusting her away from him and frowning down at her with those dark eyes suddenly harsh with anger. 'You are my wife! Not some inanimate object bought and paid for, for my own exclusive pleasure!'

'I...' She thought that was exactly what she was, and her face told him that.

'Sometimes, Nina,' he sighed as he let go of her, 'I can actually bring myself to despise you.' He turned away from her, the long body, beneath the conventional suit he was wearing, tight.

Nina shuddered, accepting that she had hurt him, and said nothing. What could she say? She still believed herself to be bought.

'I will, of course, accede to your wishes,' he continued stiffly, sounding so grim and remote that it brought fresh tears to her eyes. 'But I will not allow you to stay here alone. I will send for my mother and——'

'But I don't want your mother here!' She stared at him as if he had gone mad. Was he totally blind to his mother's dislike of her? 'I don't need her.'

'To listen to you, you don't need anyone!' he ground out, spinning back to lance her with a bitter look. 'Nevertheless,' he insisted, 'you will accede to *my* wish in this!'

His voice brooked no argument and Nina sank heavily on to a seat. 'But, w-what will she think, if y-you aren't...?'

'She will think we have a very strange relationship,' Anton mocked tightly. 'But I will attempt to console her worries by explaining that it is I who needs to be on hand at my home due to business, and not your aversion to having me anywhere near you!'

'But that isn't what I——'

'You know where I am if you find by some off chance that you need me,' he cut in brusquely, and Nina watched him miserably as, grimly, tensely, he moved to the door. 'If not,' he added as he reached it, turning to glance coldly at her forlorn figure slumped in the chair, 'I will come tomorrow, with my mother.'

His mother arrived, cold, stiff, and so obviously under protest that Nina smiled bleakly to herself and showed her to the guest-room.

It was Sadie who brought her the letter much later that same day. 'I forgot all about it in the panic over your father,' she apologised as she handed it to her. 'It came while you were away.'

Nina gazed down at the familiar black scratchy handwriting, hesitating uncertainly before, with reluctant fingers, she broke the seal, and within seconds was trembling with loathing.

It was a hard, hurting, soul-destroying letter. A letter in which all Jason's pain and contempt spilled out in a hot lava flow of bitter hatred gone so deep that Nina could only stand in the middle of her bedroom, locked in the horror of his terrible lies. He had brutally dissected her with his bitterness, her father, and worst of all, her mother. He had written such vile lies about her mother, lies that made her feel sick to her stomach, and ripped away every last ounce of feeling she had left for him.

She and my father were lovers. Had been for years before your father found out. He knew I knew, and was so terrified that I might tell you what a faithless bitch you had for a mother that he made it easy for me to make him pay for my silence. And you made it easier for me to keep on the pressure by being so sweetly gullible to every lie I handed you. He hated seeing me with you, having to watch as another of his women was taken from him by a Hunter. It really stuck in his throat, and I enjoyed watching him choke on it.

Your mother was leaving you to come to us the night she died. Jonas never forgave my father for that. He ruined my father to get his precious revenge on him. And I wanted to ruin him in return. I would have succeeded, too, if that damned Greek hadn't messed it all up. He wanted Lovell's for himself, but I stood in his way. Until he came along, you were mine for the taking. Just as your mother was my father's for the taking. She was nothing without my father. And my father was nothing without Jonas Lovell. He died a miserable failure, and I wanted to see your father go the same way. He had it coming to him. I was going to take it all: Lovell's, his money, his pride and his precious daughter.

I wanted you to know all this, before I leave this damned country for good. Your Greek paid me well enough to make that possible, but not well enough to buy my silence. So, consider this my parting gift to you, my dear Nina. The truth, written down in black and white.

The paper crackled as her fingers screwed tightly around it. The sheer ignominy of it all quivered sickeningly through her. There was more, much more, but she couldn't read on, didn't need to to know how the letter became more objectionable, more abusive. She was able to forgive Jason almost anything after the cruel way she had treated him, but not this, not these awful malignant lies that were already beginning to eat away at her even as she utterly rejected them, and, on a muffled choke, she got up, the awful letter rending in two as she ran, trembling, to her bathroom so she could be sick.

For the next few days, she devoted all of her time to her father, avoiding Ianthe as much as she could, though she had to be grateful for the cool, efficient way her mother-in-law kept the house running smoothly around them, answering all telephone calls, all enquires about Jonas Lovell's health, and, in general, easing Nina of any burden that did not involve her father's well-being.

And Jason's letter was not as difficult to put out of her mind as she thought it would be, when another entirely new problem began to worry her. One which might have begun with Jason's letter, but had not abated since. She was having to be sick each morning, and her body warned her to fear the worst. She could be pregnant with Anton's baby, and she didn't know how she was going to tell him.

Now that the first flush of passion was over, the man she had come to love so completely had become a stranger again. He seemed averse to even coming close to her.

How did you tell a man like that that you might be going to have his child?

So, once again, their ever-changing relationship took on a new pattern. She would hear his silver Mercedes draw up with a crunch of tyres on gravel each evening, and her heart would give a pathetic leap of pleasure, but she didn't move from her father's side, which was where Anton would find her, coming to stand silent and grim while he studied Jonas Lovell's wasted face before taking a firm grip on her arm to take her firmly from the room. Then he and his mother could preside over her like a pair of disapproving judges while she ate a decent meal, then he would get up and leave them, going into her father's study to deal with anything there was which might require attention, before leaving the house altogether.

No kisses, not even a soothing embrace. Ianthe's onerous presence dissuaded her from making any attempt to heal the breach growing wider and wider between them with each passing day. Feeling empty inside, she would return to her father, to stay there until the nurse came to take over from her so she could get some sleep. And another day would slip by without her sharing her secret with Anton, almost hugging it to herself as if the knowledge of the baby was her only comfort in her black little world.

A week later and Jonas was showing signs of improvement. He was still very weak, but could answer slurredly any questions put to him, and was no longer lying so frighteningly still as he had been doing.

Anton began spending a short time with him while Nina showered and changed for dinner, and she would come back to find them conversing in quiet, comfortable tones. It still niggled her, the way her father had so easily accepted a man who, mere months before, had been set to ruin him. It niggled her how easily she had accepted him too. Nothing fitted, nothing ever had, and she would remain quiet and withdrawn within herself, constantly struggling with it all, and still getting no real answers.

A week after that, she was smoothing a nice clean pillow behind her father's head when he suddenly reached out to grip her wrist with more strength than she had thought him capable of. 'You love him, don't you?' he demanded hoarsely. 'You do love him?'

She didn't even try to evade the question. 'Yes,' she said, smiling in such a way that Jonas could not be anything but convinced.

'Good.' His old eyes closed tiredly as he relaxed back into his pillows. 'I worried for a time that you'd married him for my sake.'

Nina took his hand in hers, feeling the ever-present lump in her throat thicken. She was going to lose him, she knew she was, he just didn't have it in him to fight his way back from this one.

Silvered lashes flicked upwards again. 'Just like your mother.' He smiled at her. 'Hair like hers, and her lovely face and pretty figure.' His eyes roamed her face for a while. 'My eyes, though,' he claimed proudly. 'You got those blue eyes from me.'

'Yes.' She managed a husky laugh. 'And your stubbornness,' she added teasingly. 'And your temper.'

'Oh, I don't know about the temper,' he argued. 'Both I and your mother had one of those. I remember when she...' His voice trailed away, eyes clouding over as his thoughts went inwards. 'She was a good woman, Nina,' he said suddenly. 'Always remember that. I loved her very much, though I may not have shown it much.'

'I know,' Nina soothed, holding back the tears.

'Perhaps if I'd actually said it to her more, she wouldn't have——'

'I think she knew,' Nina put in quickly, seeing with a slight twinge of alarm that he had begun to get agitated. 'She was just—unhappy with herself, that was all.'

'Unhappy, yes...' he sighed. 'But not always,' he claimed with an oddly bleak smile. 'A lively little thing once, your mother. Get up to all kinds of tricks. Impulsive?' He let out a soft laugh. 'The devil himself would get into her sometimes, and I used to wonder what she would do next just to torment me. We got on well then...'

Nina's smile was misty as she recalled that bright, glittering, almost hectic side of her mother's nature. It had used to frighten her a little, she remembered, her child's mind likening the brilliance to a brightly flaming torch in real danger of burning itself out—which it had in the end, she remembered sadly, snuffed out in the most tragic way possible.

'Until he took a fancy to her.'

Nina frowned. 'Who did?' she asked, wondering what she'd missed hearing him say.

'Wrecked our lives...' he mumbled restlessly. 'Wrecked his own in the end. Couldn't let him get away with it, not and live with myself. Pride.' He grimaced, and it was only then that Nina realised he was not really aware of her any more, his mind had taken off on some tangent of its own. Back into his past.

And suddenly she went very still, a fine silken thread beginning to weave several separate things together in her mind in a way which had her blood congealing in her veins.

'Damned Hunters,' he muttered, and Nina stood up abruptly, staring across the room to where her mother's portrait hung in pride of place above the fireplace in her father's bedroom, the full and true horror of what he was actually saying hitting her full in the face. 'Damned blasted Hunters wanted to take both my women away from me! Where are you going?' he demanded suddenly.

Her blue eyes flickered as she dragged them back to him. 'Nowhere,' she whispered, her heart thundering in her breast. She forced a smile on to her face.

'Sweet girl,' her father sighed. 'My sweet, sweet girl. Can't touch you now. I've seen to that.' His mouth stretched into a weak contented smile, and he slipped into sleep as he often did, with a single blink of an eye.

Nina stared across the room at the portrait of her mother, waiting while every illusory veil she had worn throughout the years was peeled painfully away.

Jason had been telling the truth in that final letter.

Her mother had been involved in a passionate affair with his father.

She had been leaving them to go to Michael Hunter the night she died.

On an anguished groan, she fled from the room, so blinded by the horrors taking form in her mind that she didn't see Ianthe and cannoned right into her.

'Nina!' she said sharply. 'Is your father all right?'

She couldn't even manage a yes, instead she just pushed past her and ran into her own room, only just making it to the bathroom before she was horribly sick.

'Take this.' A hand appeared in front of her blurred vision, holding a glass of water.

She took it in a trembling hand, feeling Ianthe's curious gaze on her as she sipped carefully at the water. 'I'll be all right now,' she said after a while, her eyes carefully guarded as she turned them on Ianthe. 'Sometimes it just gets too much,' she explained, 'w-watching him fade away like that.'

'Yes.' Her mother-in-law's tone was studiously flat, convincingly neutral. 'Do you love my son?' she asked, so unexpectedly that Nina's head shot up, eyes wide and startled for a moment.

Then she smiled wanly at the question. It seemed as if everyone wanted to know her feelings for Anton today. 'Yes,' she answered rather flatly. 'Yes, I love him.'

'Well, that has to mean something, I suppose,' Ianthe muttered, and turned and left her to her privacy.

Nina gripped the sides of the wash-basin, listening to Ianthe's quiet exit, her eyes squeezed tight shut against the pounding going on inside her head.

Poor Daddy, she thought wretchedly. Betrayed by his wife and his best friend and business partner. God, how they must have hurt him! It was no wonder he had re-fused to even speak about it.

And it was no wonder he had wanted her to have nothing to do with Jason, she added painfully. He was the man who had driven him to his first heart attack.

'And you can keep your greedy hands off my daughter as well as my company!' he'd cried out the morning all of this began. 'Neither are for the likes of you!'

Hot tears split her vision.

She had thought it was Anton who had been threatening him, but it had been Jason all along!

Every tender word, every loving gesture Jason had made towards her had just been a part of his plan to make her father pay for what he believed he'd done to his own father. He had never cared for her—only for what he could get out of the Lovells by way of revenge.

'He wants everything!' That terrible, plaintive cry of her father's reverberated around her throbbing head. 'You, Lovell's, my self-respect, everything!'

Something shuddered inside her. But it had nothing to do with Jason's duplicity, nor was it even the shock of her mother's errant behaviour which caused such a violent reaction inside her. It was the hard realisation that she had gone to plead with the wrong man on that awful rainy night months ago!

Slowly, she lifted her pained gaze to the mirror above the wash-stand, seeing clearly for herself the ravages taking place on her face as every carefully structured image she had had of Jason and Anton went through a complete metamorphosis right in front of her.

Anton had been completely innocent of every crime she'd thrown at him.

Or was he? a small, anguished voice questioned inside her head.

Her stomach revolted, and she swallowed wretchedly. Anton, like Jason, had wanted something from the Lovells and had been prepared to go to any lengths to get it.

Was there much to choose between them?

She thought not. She had still been used. Bought by one man, sold by another. And all for the sake of a silly old man's pride, and his desire to keep his wife's memory spotless for his daughter's eyes.

'My mother tells me you were—ill today.'

Nina looked irritably at the two grim faces frowning at her from across the dinner table, then looked away again. She didn't want to talk, or even pretend everything was all right, when it had to be obvious from her face that everything certainly was not. It had taken all the courage she had to come down here tonight, and worse, walk back into her father's bedroom later that afternoon as if nothing out of the ordinary had taken place. He had helped, by seeming to have forgotten their earlier conversation.

'If you are feeling unwell,' Anton persisted carefully, 'then you should speak to the doctor. There may be something——'

'I'm fine,' she put in flatly, wishing he would shut up, just ignore her as he usually did, leave her alone with the confusion of thoughts going around and around inside her head. She didn't need...

'Nina...' His hand came out to cover hers. 'This isn't doing——'

'I'm all right, I tell you!' she snapped, standing up with a jerk, fingers as cold as ice and trembling as she dragged them out from beneath his.

Face white, the strain of the last few weeks doubled in just a few short excruciating hours, she stared at the two dark faces studying her, and wondered just how much of all this they actually knew.

Anton's face told her nothing, cold, grim, as it always was these days. She felt the beginnings of a hot flush of distress creep beneath her skin, and turned away, stumbling a little in her eagerness to get out of the room before she broke down in front of them.

He caught up with her in the hall. Taking a firm grip on her arm, he marched her into her father's study and closed the door firmly behind them.

'Now,' he said, letting go of her so she whirled away to stand, hugging herself, by her father's big old desk. 'Perhaps, with the histrionics out of the way, you will explain that rude outburst just now?'

No answer. She didn't have one, and just stood there trembling instead, her glorious hair quivering against her slender back.

Anton studied her angrily for a while, then let out a long sigh. 'Nina...' he appealed more gently, keeping his distance from her, as if he could sense how brittle her control was, and didn't want to shatter it completely. 'What's wrong? Can't you tell me?'

He actually sounded as though he needed her to, and her heart lurched in helpless yearning to do just that and pour the whole sorry mess out to him. But she had made that silly mistake before, and look where it had got her: married to a man who might never feel more for her than desire.

'Is it all getting too much for you?' he persisted when she said nothing. 'Would it be easier if I employed another nurse to help you with——'

'I don't want it making any easier,' she interrupted thickly, 'I just want leaving alone.'

Another silence stretched between them. 'Has your father said something to upset you?' he then asked carefully. 'My mother said you came rushing out of his room as though something or someone had upset you deeply.'

She turned at that, the terrible bleakness in her gaze drawing in the tense corners of her mouth. 'He's dying, you know.'

'Yes.' Anton didn't even try to pretend otherwise. 'I know.'

He looked beautiful. And her love for him spilled into the anguished blue of her eyes. Even here, in the dim fusty atmosphere of her father's old-fashioned study, she felt her lonely senses reach out towards him. This man who had given her so much, yet never offered her more than the unhidden heat of his passion in return.

But even that was missing from his dark brown eyes now.

She looked down and away, knowing what she had always known, that when the hot sting of desire left him there would be nothing else left to hold him to her.

Except a baby, maybe. The tiniest flutter of hope made a desperate attempt to draw life inside her. Would their child hold him to her? Would he love her then? Could he love her then?

Or would a child only tie him more indelibly to a woman he'd been forced to marry by the insatiable clutch of his own loins and the desperate straits of a sick old man.

She drew herself up, forcing her eyes to level with his. She had to know if he felt anything for her other than the lust he had never denied. 'Y-you made a promise to me once,' she began huskily. 'You s-said our commitment to one another would end the day my father dies.'

'Ah.' It was his turn to lower his gaze, a strange smile that told her nothing touching the grim contours of his mouth. 'And you are now calling in that promise.' Not a question, but a grim statement of fact.

'I n-need to know if that agreement still stands,' she explained.

'So you can make plans?' The eyes flicked back to her. 'So you can, perhaps, go back to your music-loving Jason?'

'No!' She shuddered at the very thought. 'I—I never want to lay eyes on him again. He——'

'Good.' Anton said, cutting her off before she could even begin to explain why she'd had such a complete change of heart about Jason Hunter. 'Because he is the one man I would never let you leave me for.'

'But you will let me go to anyone else?' She smiled ruefully at the idea, and so did he, the same bitter twist of a thing that held no humour.

'That all depends,' he drawled, pausing to study the wretched anxiety in her guarded blue eyes, 'on whether you are pregnant or not.'

CHAPTER TEN

NINA'S slender frame jerked in an uncontrolled response. 'W-what do you m-mean?' she stammered, lashes flickering as she forced herself to meet his black, probing gaze.

'I didn't bother taking any precautions against such an event—did you?' said Anton.

A small shake of her head gave him his answer, eyes searching his face in an attempt to read his expression. He couldn't know, she told herself anxiously, he just couldn't...

'Why not?' he wanted to know. 'Because of your father?' he suggested cynically. 'Was that to be your final sacrifice for him, Nina? To grant his wish for a grandson before he died?'

'No!' She shook her head again, denying that absolutely. She had thought about guarding herself against getting pregnant, then, in the end, done nothing about it. But not because her father wanted it. The trouble was, she couldn't actually say what had made her disregard the need for protection, except maybe because some deep inner part of her already knew, well before she married Anton, that she loved him, and it had wanted to have at least a small part of him to hold on to when the inevitable happened, and he tired of her.

'But a child could be possible,' he persisted thoughtfully, eyes narrowing on her, faintly challenging, giving nothing of himself away. 'When was the last time we made love?' he mused, 'Ah, yes,' he said. 'I remember...'

The moment he began speaking in that soft silky voice, needle-sharp tingles of awareness started piercing the thick shell of self-defence she had grown around herself to guard against both him and his addictive sensuality, and she straightened warily, knowing what he was going to say.

'Two weeks and three days ago to be exact.' He began walking across the few yards' gap between them, 'It was very early in the morning, just as my hot Greek sun was rising above the villa, and you decided it would be fun to taunt me a little with your beautiful body.' His hands came up to mould her shoulders, and she began to tremble. 'You seduced me,' he said, taunting her with the mocking smile on his lips.

Nina closed her eyes, her traitorous mind conjuring up the pictures he was cruelly calling up, of a wild moment when she had woken him up from a contented sleep to insist he walk with her up the hill at the back of the villa so they could watch the sun rise. Up there, overlooked only by the sea and the trees and the slow lifting of the sun, she had seduced him, using every sensual wile he had taught her to bring his body into full throbbing life.

'How could I ever forget that wanton creature who spun her magic spell around me that morning?' he sighed, the sensual rasp of his breath on her face sending tiny white-hot shivers chasing across the surface of her skin. 'A woman whose searching lips paid homage to my body. Whose hair became a cloak of living flame around my face as she rode me out into the heavens, defying the gods, her silken limbs urging me onwards, forever upwards——'

'Stop it,' she breathed, shaken to her very depths by the quick-fire sensual flow he was so easily creating inside her.

'Could we have seeded our child that morning, *matia mou*?' he wondered throatily, his body so close to hers that it took all her will-power not to arch invitingly to him, just as she had that magical morning. 'It would be a glorious beginning for him if we did, would it not? Forging a life beneath the stinging heat of a hot Greek sun. His mother turned fiery goddess, while I...' he paused to make her quiver at the beauty of his rueful smile '...I the lowly mortal, lost in her wild enchantment.'

'No,' she groaned, hating him for reminding her, making her vulnerable to him all over again. 'No,' she said again, dragging in a shaky breath of air. 'It—it isn't possible.'

'Not possible?' Silkily he questioned her certainty. 'But surely, anything, my fiery enchantress, was possible that day.'

'Not th-that.' she denied, and her stomach quivered, as if the child itself wanted to acknowledge his father's claim. 'It—it was the wrong time.' She knew exactly which moment it was they had conceived their child. Not the morning Anton wished it to be, but another, far more devastating moment, on the very first night he took her tumbling over into womanhood. That, she was sure, was the moment he had laid his child in her, and she lifted her eyes to tell him just that, but the cold hardness she saw enter his cleaved her tongue to the roof of her mouth.

'That's a relief,' he said, all sensual mockery suddenly wiped clean from his voice. 'Your body I am happy to use to satiate the desires that run between us. But as a vessel for my child?' He shook his black head, watching with a kind of grim detachment her hot face blanch a sickly white. 'I want no child of mine conceived by a woman who is already planning her exit from my life barely two months after she entered it!'

Caught in the trap of her own making, Nina could only stand and stare as he lifted his hands from her as though the closeness repulsed him, and knew, as every vestige of hope withered inside her, that he would never love her. Not now, not ever. No man could utter such cruel words and feel even the smallest amount of love.

She might still excite his body—she had just seen proof of that glowing in the blackness of his eyes. But she would never touch his heart.

'And as for any decisions about your future,' he continued grimly as he turned abruptly and made for the door, 'shall we set them aside until your father is actually gone?' His harshly critical tone cut right into her, and she flinched. 'It seems the more—respectful thing to do, don't you think?'

They didn't have to wait long.

Early the following afternoon, Jonas Lovell had another heart attack. It happened without warning, only a vague restlessness about him that wasn't enough to prepare Nina for what was to come. Dr Martin arrived swiftly, called for by the nurse who read the signs. He was lying very still, barely conscious or aware of what was going on around him. Nina stood at the end of the bed, arms folded tightly across herself as cold fear and dread began to creep slowly over her.

'Nina,' Jonas called out weakly.

'Yes, Daddy.' She was beside him in an instant, the doctor's grim expression telling her there was little he could do. 'I'm here,' she quavered, taking his frail hand between hers, her pale features finely drawn against the onset of what was to come.

'Anton will look after you, sweetheart,' he whispered. 'You, Lovell's, you'll be all right with him.'

'Don't talk like that,' she scolded, trembling. 'This is just a small setback. In a few days you will be growling at me all over again.' A weak smile touched his bloodless mouth, and her eyes blurred with tears. 'I love you, Daddy,' she choked, lifting his hand and holding it there against her paste-white cheek.

The fingers flexed and curved, gently stroking the smooth, pale skin beneath them. 'Just like your mother,' he whispered threadily.

Tears washed her vision. 'No,' she groaned, knowing it was the end, yet unable to accept it. 'Daddy?' she whispered thickly, pleading with her shimmering eyes that he open his own and look at her. 'Daddy, listen to me. I have something to tell you!' Nothing, not even a small twitch of his mouth to say he had heard her. 'I am going to have a baby, Daddy!' she cried out urgently, moving her cheek so she could kiss his fingertips. 'I'm going to have a baby! Your grandson! So you have to get better, don't you? You have to——'

'Nina...' The doctor's hand coming gently around her arm felt like the cold clutch of hopelessness, and she quivered at it. 'It's all over, dear,' he broke to her, gently removing her from the bed. His voice sounded rough in the terrible silence in the room. 'It's all over, I'm sorry.'

'He didn't even hear me,' she whispered tragically.

'He heard you,' Dr Martin assured her, watching, with a fierce lump in his throat, her eyes fill with tears. 'I'm sure he did.'

'Nina——?'

The sound of that deep, familiar voice had her spinning around in search of its owner. Anton was standing just inside the bedroom door, his dark face white and grim. Through her glazed vision, she saw him glance questioningly at the doctor, felt the grim negative response emanating back from him, and it came then, the hard rasping choke of grief that shook her whole body and brought Anton striding over to her, his arms folding her in a crushing embrace.

That was the first night in almost a month that she slept in her husband's arms. While the house readied itself for mourning, Anton stayed with her in her room, absorbing her pain and grief until eventually exhaustion sent her tumbling into sleep.

She didn't wake again until deep into the night, finding herself cocooned in the warmth and comfort of his arms.

'All right?' he asked when he noticed she was awake. Nina lifted her dulled blue eyes to his. He had not slept; she could see the alertness in the grim cast of his face.

'Yes,' she breathed, and lowered her gaze from his, feeling thankfully numb inside now. 'How did you know to come?'

'My mother called me,' he explained. 'I'm sorry I couldn't make it before he——'

'He believed we loved each other, did you know that?' A small sob which was supposed to be a laugh broke in her throat. 'He died believing you the big white hero, come here to save his company and his daughter in his final hour!'

The hand curving around her tensed slightly. 'But you know otherwise, I suppose,' he sighed.

'I know the truth,' she said flatly.

'And what is the truth?' the man holding her enquired grimly.

I was bought, she thought, and moved away from him, feeling the coldness of loss sweep over her once again. Anton might have helped save her father's company from Jason's greedy hands, and she would always be grateful to him for that. But she had sold herself to him to get his help.

She found no solace in any of that, none at all.

He made a movement beside her as if to draw her back into his arms, and she tensed as she waited, every aching pore in her going out towards him in miserable yearning. She loved him so much! Needed so badly for him to love her too!

The tears flooded her eyes again, and she bit down hard on her quivering bottom lip, not wanting to cry, refusing to cry, feeling so lost and alone, it hurt almost as much as her father's going.

Then the arms were gathering her in anyway, and she went. Like a weak little kitten she went, curling herself into that warm hard body and burying her face in the scented hollow of his shoulder.

Just this one last time, she told herself weakly. Just let me lie here in his arms and inhale that warm musky smell of him this one last time.

She might never allow herself the beauty of it again.

'Nina . . .' His voice was low and roughened, sending threatening sparks of something she refused to acknowledge skidding out across her skin.

'Don't talk,' she whispered pleadingly. 'Please, don't talk.'

Jonas Lovell was buried one still morning a week later. Ianthe stood to one side of her, her manner towards Nina softened slightly by her grief. Anton stood on the other, his arm supportive around her slender waist.

He had hardly left her alone since her father's death, his mood quietly sympathetic but grim. He had taken over one of the other guest-bedrooms, and not even Ianthe questioned why he wasn't sleeping with his wife when she, like everyone, could see how utterly exhausted Nina was now the physical caring for her father was over.

And if she lay awake deep into the dark night, shivering with loneliness and a stark yearning to feel his warm body infuse some life into her own numbed one, then at least no one else knew it.

It was too late. Her father had gone now, and taken with him her right to hold on to the man she loved.

Except for their baby, an insistent little voice in her heart kept prompting urgently. Surely their child gave her the right to hold on somewhere?

She must have trembled, because Anton's arm became more supportive around her waist. 'Let's go,' he murmured, turning her gently from the grave side, and she felt Ianthe's hand rest on her shoulder for a brief moment before it was withdrawn again.

Sympathy? she wondered blankly. And wanted to sob her heart out.

The chauffeur-driven limousine took them back to the house, leading a cavalcade of funeral cars containing people who had been friends of her father's, business colleagues, people who, though they were virtual strangers to her, helped to instil a small ball of comfort inside her because they cared enough for Jonas Lovell to break off from their busy day to attend his funeral. She said as much to the man sitting beside her.

'Your father was a well-liked and deeply respected man,' Anton replied sombrely. 'Of course they cared enough to pay their respects to him. He will be sadly missed.'

The slight hint of censure in his voice sent her sliding back behind her cloak of withdrawal, and they finished the rest of the journey in silence. But the moment they entered the house Ianthe took one look at her pale, drawn face and sent her firmly to her room, and Nina went, glad of the excuse not to have to put on a brave face in front of all those people, leaving Anton and his mother to entertain them in her absence.

He found her still in her room hours later. Black coat, hat and shoes discarded, she was sitting in the window seat, her cheek resting on her drawn-up knees as she gazed sightlessly out of the window.

'You have not packed,' he observed as he stepped inside the room and closed the door.

Nina turned her head as he spoke, running the question through her mind several times before its meaning sank in. He was expecting her to return with him to his home today.

'I'm not coming,' she said.

He stopped mid-stride, his gaze sharpening on her, then he grimaced. 'I suspected as much. May I be allowed to enquire why?' he drawled sarcastically.

'I read my father's will,' she informed him flatly.

'Ah,' he said, as if that explained it all when, really, it was only the very tip of the iceberg encasing her.

'He had a copy in his bedside drawer. I found it while I was clearing out his personal things. He left you everything,' she concluded heavily.

'Yes,' he sighed, sitting down on the end of the bed. 'In trust,' he made it clear. 'For our first-born son. But I hope you will believe me when I say I didn't know he was going to do that.'

'It doesn't matter,' she murmured indifferently. She actually understood why her father had done it. He had believed he was protecting her from any other Jason Hunters who might think it worth preying on his daughter's naïveté. 'He owed it to you, anyway,' she shrugged, thinking, What a pathetic person I must be to make my own father go to such lengths to protect me.

'Of course it damn well matters!' Anton exploded gruffly. 'I wanted none of it!'

'You wanted Lovell's.'

'I wanted you, Nina. And I refuse to let you forget that fact.'

He wanted her... She remembered the first time he'd ever said that to her, here in this very room, what seemed an age ago now.

With her pale cheek still resting on her upturned knees, she let her eyes run over him. His posture was heavy, the stresses of the last few weeks beginning to affect him also. Something fluttered inside her, and she damped it down hard, refusing to give it space to grow.

He looked up suddenly, catching her gaze, and for once she didn't look away. It was a slate-grey September day outside. Her own curled-up figure was blocking most of the natural light from the room. She couldn't see his face clearly, but could sense his grimness. The mood in the room was grim, the air they breathed, the words they spoke.

'It is time to come home, Nina,' Anton stated quietly, refusing to accept her earlier refusal.

'No.' Home to her was a sun-kissed island a million miles away from here. It had been the only place she had found happiness recently. Straightening her stiffened limbs, she got up. 'I—I need some time to be by myself,' she insisted, hugging herself as if cold.

'What is that supposed to mean?' His body was stiff as he stood up too.

Nina turned away from the aching beauty of his tall, lean frame, an unwanted need to simply throw herself at him almost overwhelming her. 'I need time to think, plan what I am going to do with my life now.'

'You are coming home with me!' he stated arrogantly, sounding so utterly Greek that she almost smiled. 'Where you will take up your responsibilities as my wife again!'

'In your bed, I suppose you mean.'

'Yes, in my bed,' he snapped, reaching out for her to pull her around to face him. 'Wife, lover—what's the difference? It is your place. To be with me, wherever I am, not living and sleeping separately!'

'But my father is dead!'

'Yes.' He nodded curtly, fingers tightening on her upper arms. 'And I respect your grief, but from now on you will grieve in my home! I will not tolerate this foolish separation any longer! God knows,' his breath rasped her face on an angry sigh, 'I should not have let this begin in the first place! But now it is time to put an end to it. And you, Nina Lakitos, are to come home with me. Today!'

'But you promised to free me of any commitments to you on my father's death!' Just tell me that you love me, Anton, she pleaded wretchedly inside, and I'll walk over hot coals to be anywhere with you! 'We talked about it, only a few nights ago, and you promised——'

'To discuss it,' he cut in grimly. 'And discuss it we will, at home—our home!'

His angry insistence alone made her want to give in to him. She wanted to let him take the weight of her worries from her shoulders, let her hide behind the strength of his autocratic will. But it wouldn't be right. Not any more. Not with her father dead and their bargain finished. She was pregnant with his child, and she needed more than just his desire for her as a woman now. She needed desperately, his love.

'Please...' she pleaded with the dark anguish in her eyes, head back, hair tumbling in wild disarray down her back and with no idea how tragically beautiful she looked to the man glaring right back at her. 'Try to understand! I can't just walk back into things as they were before!'

'And what were they?' he challenged. 'A man and a woman barely setting out on learning about each other! And you want to throw it all away because—because of what?' He actually looked confused as his black eyes pierced angrily into hers.

'B-because it was part of our bargain.'

'Just a silly pact,' he dismissed with contempt. 'Made to salve your guilty conscience because you wanted me so badly that you abhorred yourself for it!'

'That isn't true!' she denied, knowing inside that it was the exact truth.

'It isn't?' His gaze sliced darkly over her, raising the fine sensitive hairs on the back of her neck as it went. 'Let us just test that theory, shall we?' And before she could even think what he meant to do, he pulled her angrily against the hard tension of his body.

His mouth came cruel and punishing on top of her own with a kiss that burned itself into the very depth of her being and swung her away on a hot current of ruthlessly incited sensuality which left her nothing—nothing of herself to salvage from it.

'The truth,' he jeered as he pushed her away, breaking the kiss so abruptly that she stood there swaying in front of him, staring at the scathing mask of his contempt with her mind still lost in a whirling pleasure. 'What do you know about the truth, when you have such an unerring ability to tie the truth into knots just to suit your own purposes?'

He turned away from her, striding tensely for the door. 'Stay here if that is what you want to do!' he decided bitterly. 'But this is the last time I walk away from this house without you,' he warned as he reached it, turning to flay her with a last bitter look. 'You know where I am if you change your mind. Just pray to yourself that I will not have changed *my* mind by then!'

With the hard slamming of the door, he was gone, leaving her wondering dazedly just what she had been hoping for as her heart split wide open to allow all her pain to ooze out, and, on a broken sob, she threw herself down on her bed, crouching there to cry, cry as she had never done before. She cried for herself, for her father, for the child she carried so secretly inside her, and even for the man who had just walked so angrily from her life.

The sudden sharp knocking at the door brought her jerking into a sitting position, her heart giving a pathetic leap in her breast.

It is not Anton, she told herself hectically as she scrambled off the bed. He said he wouldn't come back, and he won't.

And it wasn't.

Nina had barely managed to dry the tears from her wet cheeks before the bedroom door was opening to allow Ianthe to walk in on her.

'Nina!' she cried, looking more anxious than angry. 'Why has my son just stormed out of here in a black rage?'

Nina turned away, moving back to the window again, hiding, hiding as she always seemed to do these days. 'Why don't you go and ask him, Ianthe?' she suggested dully. 'It is his feelings you are most concerned about, after all.'

In all her life, she had never felt so lost and alone, and it must have shown in the bleak quality of her voice, because, contrary to her expectations, Ianthe did not come back at her spitting her usual contempt, but sighed heavily instead, and came to stand right beside her, a gentle hand reaching out to touch her arm.

'Aye, aye, aye,' she sighed in tragic dismay. 'Have you not enough grief to contend with at the moment, Nina, without bringing more upon yourself by alienating my son?' The arm beneath Ianthe's touch trembled, and she sighed yet again. 'I thought you assured me that you loved him,' she persisted softly. 'Why is it, then, that I have had to watch the way you are slowly breaking his heart?'

His heart? Nina thought bitterly. What heart? And what about my heart? The tears came back to her blue eyes. 'Anton doesn't have a heart,' she derided thickly, 'He has a slab of rock in its place!'

'Oh?' Far from being offended by the insult, Ianthe's voice actually gentled even more! 'And have you ever bothered trying to prove that statement to yourself?'

'I know what I know,' she mumbled.

'I suppose, by that, you are referring to your father's company being the only reason my son went against his mother's wishes by marrying you?'

'I am talking about lust, Ianthe,' Nina was stung into replying, not caring what she said any more. Things had gone way beyond the need for pretence now. 'It was the only way he could get me into his bed, so he married me!'

She felt Ianthe go stiff beside her. 'Then, if you agreed to marry him knowing that, why are you not using every ploy you know to keep those lusts alive, rather than sending him away as you obviously must have done?'

'I... You just wouldn't understand,' she sighed, watching the steadily dying grey light outside fade into a miserable darkness.

'You perhaps expected more than Anton offered you?'

'No.' Nina even managed a small smile at that suggestion. 'I never expected more than he offered me.'

'But, because you love him, you automatically expect him to love you in return,' Ianthe assumed.

Feeling empty inside, Nina turned away to go and sit down heavily on the chair beside her bed. Not once had she ever expected him to love her, she thought bleakly. Wished for it maybe, but never expected it.

Ianthe remained where she was, studying her for a while as the room grew steadily darker, then she began to move briskly around, switching on lamps, forcing the light to lift the grim atmosphere from around them. 'You know, Nina,' she said as she moved about, 'love does not come with the blinding flash of wonder the romantics would like us to believe. It takes time and careful nurturing to grow. It means working hard at getting to know someone, learning their likes and dislikes, making them feel so content to be with you that they could not even consider looking elsewhere for consolation. I should know,' she murmured rather drily, coming to sit down on the bed, and reaching out to grasp Nina's cold hands in hers.

'My own marriage was not a love-match as you English like to describe the union,' she admitted, the wry twist of her lips bringing Nina's gaze jumping to meet hers in surprise. 'The Greeks do things differently from you,' she explained. 'I was just sixteen when my father first introduced me to my future husband, and I hated him on the spot.' The smile became a grimace. 'He was fifteen years older than I, and so frighteningly sophisticated that I thought him old and stuffy—told him so too!' She laughed softly at the memory. '"Then you must teach me how not to be stuffy, must you not, Ianthe?" he said to me, and cleverly laid down a challenge I was more than willing to take up.' Black eyes came up to level with vulnerable blue. 'He made me fall in love with him first, Nina, then made me work even harder at earning his love.'

'And did you?' Her voice was hoarse, and Nina had to clear the lump of pathetic hope from her throat before she could go on. 'Did you make him love you?'

The older woman's face had softened into something almost beautiful as she talked about her late husband, but her gaze remained solemn on Nina. 'A Greek man,' she began by way of a reply, 'is different from any race of men in the world. Do not, Nina, expect more from my son than you are prepared to give, or he will always disappoint you. Hide your feelings behind your pride if you must, run away from them if you have to. But if you do, then do not then live in the thankless hope that he will some day come and lay his heart at your feet, because he will never do it. You say my son only married you to satiate his lust,' she went on grimly. 'Then, is that not enough to begin the fight for more? Or is, perhaps, your own love not strong enough to support you in the fight?'

Nina looked down at her lap where her fingers lay buried beneath Ianthe's darker, much, much stronger ones. 'Why are you bothering with all of this?' she questioned huskily. 'I thought it would please you to think I was letting him go.'

Ianthe's finely sculptured brows rose in full hauteur. 'You are carrying my grandchild, are you not?' Blue eyes flicked up to clash with black in startled surprise, and Ianthe smiled in grim satisfaction, the heat which spread across Nina's cheeks giving her all the confirmation she needed. 'That, above everything,' she said, 'earns my respect.'

'But not your son's,' Nina choked, and the bleak tears brimmed all over again. 'He didn't marry me to give him his sons, Ianthe,' she whispered thickly. 'He told me that himself.'

Ianthe went stiff with shock, then scorned Nina with a look. 'Rubbish!' she denounced, getting up to move impatiently away. 'If my son said something as terrible as that to you, then you would spend your time better wondering just what you had said or done to bring such an outright lie from his lips, rather than wallowing in the hurt he inflicted on you.'

'You don't understand...' Nina sighed.

'I understand enough to know that if you do not do something positive about your relationship with Anton then it will soon reach a very hapless end.' She turned her grim face on Nina. 'Think about it, my dear,' she advised. 'There are plenty of other women out there, more than willing to help him forget all about you. Is that what you really want?'

Want? Nina wondered unhappily as Ianthe left her alone. How was she supposed to know what she wanted when she was so confused that she could barely put two coherent thoughts together?

Fight, Ianthe had advised her. But she didn't know whether she did have the strength to take such a huge battle on. And did she really want to commit herself so completely to a man who only wanted her because her body excited him?

It would not be many months before the lithe and slender figure he so loved to eat with his eyes would be blown out of all proportion, growing big with the child they had made between them. Would he even want to look at her then?

And there was another grim consideration. She loved this baby already, and would kill to keep it safe. But if she decided she could not live with Anton without his love, would he try to take the baby away from her? If it was a son, then he would be Anton's heir. His Greek nature surely would not allow his own son to live separately from him?

She could of course just quietly disappear from his life. Move away, go and live...

Live where? Go where? Her heart wrenched at the utter bleakness of it all. She knew where she wanted to be. Love or not, wanted or not. She knew exactly where she yearned to be.

CHAPTER ELEVEN

SEPTEMBER was curling its way out of the year on dry misty frosts that put a silver haze over the orange street lamps and turned the ground black and hard.

Nina stood just inside the pair of wrought-iron gates, staring at the white-rendered mansion house. Unlike the first time she had stood here like this, the house seemed at peace, no cars filling the driveway, no sound of music drifting towards her.

She pulled the collar of her warm woollen coat closer to her throat, trembling slightly as she began moving forwards, still unsure if she was doing the right thing, but, as on the first time she made this journey, she had to see the man inside, talk to him.

'Is...your own love not strong enough to support you in the fight?' Ianthe had challenged.

Well, she had come here to find that out.

Heart beating a little too unevenly for comfort, she stepped up to the front door and rang the bell. She was afraid, she had to admit it, afraid of his welcome, or if he would welcome her at all.

'You know where I am if you change your mind!' he'd snapped at her. She could only hope and pray he meant it.

The door swung inwards, golden light spilling out from the hallway to show John Calver standing there, his expression startled before he managed to mask it.

'Hello, John,' she said, stepping past him into the inner vestibule.

'Mrs Lakitos,' he greeted her politely, hesitating slightly before closing the door, then moving around to

170

stand in front of her, almost as though he were trying to block her progress into the house.

'Is my husband at home?' She looked at him curiously, wondering if that was the reason for his odd behaviour. Perhaps Anton hadn't even waited one day before going out to seek that solace his mother mentioned. Perhaps...

'Yes, of course.' His eyes went flickering across the hall towards the closed study door then came guardedly back to Nina. 'If—if you'll just wait here a moment, I'll——'

'No.' She stopped him with a hand as he went to stride away, sending him a dry smile when he glanced warily at her. 'If you don't mind, John, I would rather announce myself.' She didn't want Anton pre-warned, she wanted to see for herself his initial reaction at finding her here. It could tell her everything she needed to know. Swallowing tensely, she lifted her gaze across the hall. 'Is he in his study?'

'Yes, but...' He seemed uncertain of what he should do, then, on a shrug, offered to take her coat instead of arguing any further.

'Thank you.' She relinquished the black wool coat to reveal a simple black silk knit dress beneath, then walked across the polished wood floor towards the study, aware of John Calver's tense gaze on her all the way, but too nervous to be curious about it.

At the door, she paused, taking a moment to quell the hectic hammer of her heart, then, on a determined lift of her chin, turned the handle and stepped quietly into the room, her eyes flicking quickly around the strange surroundings until they settled on the man who was standing just in front of a paper scattered desk.

And everything inside her shuddered to a halt as the icy clutch of a hand closed tightly around her heart.

He wasn't alone. Louisa was with him, her slender body leaning intimately against his, her arms wound possessively around his neck in much the same way as Nina had seen them before. Anton was smiling indulgently into her eyes, his mouth curved in that sensual smile Nina recognised only too well.

They were so engrossed in each other that they hadn't even heard her enter. 'I can't believe it is happening at last!' Louisa was saying excitedly.

Anton smiled down at her. 'Well, it is about time someone made an honest woman out of you, minx,' he teased, and lowered his mouth to Louisa's waiting one.

The hand clutching at her heart let go suddenly, allowing the pain it had been holding in such tight restraint to spring outwards in a jarring wave that had Nina swaying dizzily. She must have made a sound of pain, because Anton glanced up at that moment, their eyes clashing over the top of Louisa's dark head, his showing a total disbelief for one split second before he was pushing Louisa from him with such force that the action screamed guilt.

'Nina!' he breathed in stunned amazement.

Louisa's startled head shot around to stare at her, her olive skin burning up with a guilty colour that only helped to condemn them both, and Nina turned away, stumbling a little in her eagerness to leave the room, get out of here before they witnessed the total degeneration of everything she had left inside her.

But before she could move further than the open doorway, a strong hand closed on her elbow, 'Don't be stupid, Nina,' Anton murmured gruffly. 'This isn't what you——'

'You are every awful thing I ever thought of you, aren't you?' she cried, pulling at her captured arm.

He muttered something nasty beneath his breath, trying to keep her still in front of him while she struggled to get free.

'Stop it!' he bit out tightly.

'Let me go!' With panic blurring any sense she might have left, she moved desperately, tugging at her arm again, and this time Anton made the mistake of letting her go, because she turned on him like a wild thing, only becoming aware of what she had done when she heard the shrill sound of a slap, and the stinging heat of her palm told her it had collided with something warm and hard!

His entire body jerked under the force of the blow, his eyes growing murderous for the moment it took him to control the urge to slap her back, then silence fell around them, broken only by the shallow gasps of her own hectic breathing while he stood there with the white-lined marks of her fingers firmly imprinted on to the side of his face.

'Your—penchant for causing me bodily harm has raised its ugly head again, I see,' he bit out tightly, pulsing with a fury she hadn't witnessed since their first explosive meeting in the all-consuming darkness of his bedroom months ago.

'Y-you deserved it!' she spat out furiously, hot tears pressing at the backs of her eyes, her heart hammering way out of control as she stood there, hating him with every wounded part of her, 'You deserve everything you get!' she choked, and spun away from him, needing to get out of here, having to get out of here before she——!'

Her wrist was caught in a steely manacle of a grip, pulling her to a mid-flight halt, sending her hair flying out wildly as he spun her back to see the black blaze of fury burning in his eyes. 'John,' he bit out from between tightly clenched teeth. He was so angry, he was throbbing with it. 'See Miss Mandraki to her car and then get the hell out of here yourself.'

'Yes, sir.' It was only then that Nina remembered the two other people present, and she began to tremble, tremble with shock, with horror, and with a real fear that Anton was not going to let her get away with humiliating him like this in front of them.

'Anton—I . . .' Nina stiffened violently as that thick-as-cream voice began to speak. Her eyes flashed blue hatred at him all over again.

'Get out of here, Louisa,' he ordered roughly. 'I love you very dearly, but get the hell out of here. I don't need any witnesses when I commit murder!' he added silkily for Nina's benefit.

There was a short pause, filled with a throbbing silence while everyone in the hall took that last threat in, then John Calver was moving, his actions jerking Louisa into life, and they both strode off towards the front door, leaving Nina and Anton glaring angrily at each other.

A hard silence settled over the house. Nina was still trembling, the desolation she was trying desperately to hold in check forcing her to breathe in small hurried gasps. The kind of emotions darting around them were keeping every sense they possessed on stinging red alert.

'What was she doing here?' she demanded when she could stand the drumming silence no longer.

'What right have you to think you may ask that question?' he threw back bitterly.

'A wife's right!' she snapped, glaring into the angry beauty of his dark face.

'You're no wife,' he sneered. 'You never have been.'

Throwing her wrist aside, he turned away from her, striding angrily across the room to a drinks cabinet where he poured himself a large brandy.

'W-what's that supposed to mean?' she demanded, the cheek she had slapped seeming to taunt her with the angry red lines running at an angle across it.

'A child is what you are, Nina,' he said, slicing her a contemptuous glance before looking away again. 'A silly aggravating child who is more trouble than she is damned well worth!'

'If you think that,' she choked out wretchedly, 'then why did you marry me?'

'You know why.' He took a deep gulp at his drink. 'Because I couldn't keep my lecherous hands off your body.'

His derision cut right into her. 'A problem you've managed to cure, I now see,' she threw right back, having to clasp her hands tightly together in front of her they were trembling so badly.

'Don't you believe it,' he bit out, flashing her another scathing glance. 'I could drag you upstairs right now and tumble you on to the bed if it weren't for that— pathetic ethereal look you've managed to develop over the last few weeks.'

'My father has been ill!' Hurt tears filled her eyes all over again.

Black eyes glinted malevolently at her, then he sighed heavily. 'Yes,' he said. 'I know, and that was a low thrust, I apologise for it.' He took another gulp at his drink, and Nina stared bleakly at him.

He was still furiously angry, the usual rich quality of his skin lost to a pallor she had never seen on his face before, and her heart lurched achingly in her breast; he hadn't enjoyed being caught out by her like this. It had touched his pride, his self-esteem.

'I'm sorry,' she mumbled, feeling more the culprit than he for some crazy reason. 'I should have called to warn you I was coming here tonight.'

'Should you?' He sent her a strange look, then lowered his dark head to stare grimly into his glass. 'Why have you come?'

Why had she come? An empty smile touched the tight corners of her mouth. Her reasons for coming here tonight had now been rendered null and void, seeing him with Louisa had seen to that.

It was time to hide again, she realised bleakly, At least attempt to leave here with some pride still intact.

Making a firm effort to control the anguish clamouring inside her, she lifted her small chin to send him a cold stare. 'To tell you it is all over between us,' she managed to say with credible calm.

That seemed to hit a sensitive nerve somewhere, she noted as he stiffened jerkily, then grimaced, more at himself than at her. 'I suppose I should have expected that,' he murmured cynically. 'But, oddly, I didn't.'

'I—I've decided to return to college,' she told him, wanting to see him hurt as much as he had hurt her, and knowing it was a hopeless wish. She had been right earlier when she'd told his mother Anton had no heart—he hadn't.

'Ah, the all important musical studies,' he drawled, and took another sip of his drink. 'And the all important Jason, I suppose,' he then added bitterly.

She couldn't let that remark pass without correcting it. 'I know about Jason,' she informed him. 'And I know about my mother.'

That brought him swinging around to face her fully. 'How?' he asked sharply.

'Apparently, Jason didn't think you had paid enough for his silence,' she mocked acidly, then shot him a half-questioning, half-accusing look. 'He bled my father so dry that he had to go begging to his friends just to keep his head afloat, didn't he?'

He didn't answer, the averting of his grim face an acknowledgement in itself.

'And all to keep my mother's memory clean,' she sighed, sucking in a deep breath and letting it out again as the full weight of all her disillusionments settled heavily on her once again. 'It wasn't worth it. He should have known I would far rather have had him safe and happy, and my mother's image ruined, than what I have now.' The onset of grief-stricken tears showed in her voice.

'And what do you have?' he enquired grimly.

'Nothing much,' she said, looking away from him, her face ashen against the brilliance of her red-gold hair. 'An empty marriage based on an old man's frantic attempts to salvage something from the mess he had made of his life, and your insatiable lust.' She gave a bitter smile.

'Don't forget your own lusts, Nina,' Anton prompted cynically. 'It takes two very attracted people to generate the kind of sexual charge you and I manage to produce between us.'

Shame engulfed her, then she lifted her chin to him, eyes like iced blue glass. 'Which is why I have decided to return to my studies. I refuse to be used by other people ever again. You made me want you, Anton,' she added bitterly. 'I didn't want to feel like that.'

'And you think I did?' He put the glass down with a thud, the atmosphere between them so bleak that it made her shiver.

'I suppose that was all my fault too,' she sighed. 'Turning up here that night, begging like a fool for you to help us.'

'No, you are wrong there,' Anton drawled. 'It began a long time before the night you came here looking for me, Nina.'

Her heart stopped in her breast, sensing a fresh attack on the way. 'What are you talking about?' she breathed.

Anton shrugged lazily. 'I knew all about Hunter's blackmail, his attempts to inveigle you into his plans, his desire to get Lovell's for himself. I knew everything there was to know before you came to me that night— except for the engagement ring,' he added with a small smile. 'Now that was a surprise, even to me.'

'I . . .' She didn't know what to say—strange things were beginning to happen inside her. 'Why?' she asked breathlessly. 'Why did my father confide all of that in you when he was prepared to lose everything just to keep it all a secret?'

'Because he knew what I wanted,' Anton said simply, black eyes hard on her through their narrow slits. 'Which made me the only person he could trust who would be prepared to help him out of the mess he was in.'

'Me,' Nina whispered, going paler by the second.

He nodded. 'I never tried to pretend otherwise,' he reminded her. 'The night you came here looking for my help, your father already had it. We had already struck our deal,' he informed her. 'I was to get Hunter off his back with a large pay-off, and in return I was to get control over Lovell's, and you in my bed,' he told her brutally. 'Legally, of course. Your father was not about to save his daughter from the greedy clutches of one man just to land her in the lecherous ones of another.'

Nina swayed as if he had hit her. 'I hate you for that,' she choked, turning away from the hard cruelty of his smile.

'So, what's new?' he drawled, calmly refilling his glass again. 'You have always hated me, so you say. Still,' he added coolly, sliding his eyes her way as she took a trembling step towards the hallway, 'try to leave here now, Nina, and I promise you, you will be sorry.'

'Why?' she cried, spinning around to stare at him. 'Why do you still need me here when you have Louisa! Or is one woman not enough for the likes of you?'

Her angry contempt brought a flare of answering fury from him, bringing him striding across the room towards her. Nina stood her ground, chin up, eyes defiant, even while she hurt so badly he had to see it.

'One day that vile tongue of yours will get you into real trouble!' he grated, coming to a stop barely half an inch away from her to thrust his taut face up to hers.

'Then let me get out of here, and you'll never have to listen to my vile tongue again!'

'Not on your life!' he refused, a finger and thumb coming up to grab her chin and holding her hot face up to his. 'We have unfinished business, you and I,' he informed her tightly. 'The very important business of a son to keep your father's company in my control.'

Without even knowing she was doing it, her hands whipped around to cover her stomach. 'No,' she whispered shakily. 'You can't mean that!'

'You think not?' he drawled, eyes lost beneath cruelly narrowed slits. 'I have been fighting to get Lovell's in my power for too damned long to give it up now because you have decided to renege on our deal!'

'But all that died along with my father!' she cried.

'And what about our deal?' he reminded her. 'The one where you sold yourself to me body and soul?'

'That died too,' she whispered breathlessly, trembling with a real fear of him now. 'You will never father a child in me,' she thickly vowed, knowing she could never tell this cruel and ruthless man about their baby now. Never. 'I will never let you get that close to me to try!'

'Too late, my love...' he drawled softly '...when we both know my child already grows inside you.'

She swayed, her eyes closing on a dizzying wave of horror.

'You see, *matia mou*,' he persisted in a deadly voice, 'your instincts about me have been right all along. I bought you, like a slave girl in the market place, just as you always accused me of doing, and until I have everything I want from you—including that child you are so lovingly nurturing—with me is where you will stay!'

'No!' The pained negative broke from her thickened throat, while he stood watching her, his eyes black and grim, mouth set in a thin, uncompromising line that told her once and for all how little he really cared for her as a real living breathing person.

'And to think,' she whispered tremulously, staggering back from him, 'I actually believed myself to be in love with you.'

She continued to stare bleakly at him for a moment, seeing the way all the colour left his face on that last pained confession, then she turned and fled, running across the hall and grappling with the front door until she was stumbling outside, wanting to get away, having to get away before he saw the complete devastation of everything in her.

'Nina!' she heard him call out hoarsely, but she was already speeding across his lawn with no real idea of where she was going and not really caring any more.

He caught up with her when she was only halfway across his garden, his hands landing on her shoulders to pull her to a jarring halt before spinning her around to face him.

'What did you just say?' he gasped out thickly.

At last she seemed to have shaken him, she noted numbly. He looked stunned, so pale it washed all the natural richness from his skin.

'Let go of me,' she choked. 'You want to take everything from me—everything!' With an angry wrench, she managed to free herself, swirling away to come to a quivering halt three yards away from him, 'And now you want to take my baby away from me!' she sobbed out brokenly.

A spasm of real pain rippled across his stark white features. 'Nina, for God's sake . . .' he groaned. 'I didn't mean a single word of what I said back there!'

'This baby is mine to keep,' she choked, her hands covering her womb once again in fierce protection. 'And neither you nor your deals with my father are going to take it away from me!'

'I wouldn't take your child away from you, Nina,' Anton said hoarsely, his eyes strained as he watched the way she trembled. 'I was angry back there,' he sighed. 'You were talking about leaving me for good, and I retaliated. Hell!' he exploded, when she just stood there staring at him through those wide, wounded eyes. 'I have known about the baby since the day my mother said you had been ill! I even tried to make you tell me about it, but you wouldn't—would you?' And suddenly, it was his turn to be bitter, to scorn her with a look. 'You keep denying our own child to me, and wonder why I can find it in me to want to hurt you?' he choked out bitterly.

Her tumbled head shook, refusing to take responsibility for any hurt inflicted on him. 'You planned this with my father too, didn't you?' she accused. 'You planned it between you that I should get pregnant. It was just another part of your terrible bargain with him!'

Anton moved impatiently. 'There is no child on this earth I would condone being used in any deal!' he ground out harshly. 'What kind of man do you think I am that could do such an inhuman thing!'

'You used me,' she choked. 'I was only a child compared to you and my father.'

'Your father loved you, Nina,' Anton said wearily. 'He loved you so much that he was prepared to do anything to keep you safe from harm—whether it be from your mother's unsavoury past, or Hunter's greedy clutches—or my hungry ones! There is no way he would have made a deal which included you the way I implied back there.' He took in a deep breath and let it out again slowly, the colossal weight of their mutual pain clouding his grim black eyes. 'He gave me his blessing to try to make you care for me—if I could get rid of Hunter for him. But that was all,' he stated heavily. 'The rest was up to me, and I took up the challenge willingly! Nina...' he pleaded roughly, lifting a hand out between them. 'It's freezing cold out here, and you are shivering. Let's go inside so we can finish this, hmm?' he appealed. 'Please. We can——'

'I can never live with you again, Anton,' she told him, holding her place, her hair beginning to silver in the frosty night air.

'Why not?' His eyes darkened painfully. 'Because of your college studies?' he asked. 'All right!' The outstretched hand gave a dismissive flick. 'I give you back your studies!' he granted with a flash of his old arrogance. Then he added in a roughened voice, 'We are good together, you and I, Nina. You know we are. Don't throw it all away on a few crazy misunderstandings.' He took a step towards her only to groan in frustration when she fell back a couple of paces.

'You say you love me, but you will not let me even come close to you!' he rasped out angrily. 'What is it you want from me, for God's sake!'

I just want your love, she whispered wretchedly inside her head.

Silence fell between them, the crisp night air broken up by the smoky gasps of their hectic breathing. And it was only as his head came up sharply to reveal the look of shocked disbelief on his face that she realised, with a sense of horror, that she had said the words out loud!

And slowly, as the silence seemed to stretch into eternity, and still neither of them moved or spoke, Nina felt all grasp on reality begin to slip away from her.

He saw her begin to sway, and, on a broken curse, covered the space between them, snatching her back from the temptation to faint by wrapping her into a bear-hug of an embrace.

'You've always had it,' he muttered thickly into the sparkling softness of her hair. 'From the first moment I ever set eyes on you, I have been totally and irrevocably captured by you!'

'Because you desire me, that's all,' she choked, not daring to let herself believe him. It meant too much.

Anton growled impatiently, and pushed her at arm's length so he could glare at her. 'If you were not pregnant with our child,' he growled, 'if you didn't look so damned frail—I would shake the living daylights out of you, you blind stupid fool! God in heaven, Nina!' he sighed. 'Are you the only person on this earth who does not know that Anton Lakitos took one look at Jonas

Lovell's daughter and fell flat on his besotted face for her!'

'B-but Louisa——'

'Louisa is an old friend of the family,' he dismissed impatiently. 'She arrived here tonight to tell me the good news that she has just betrothed herself to another mutual friend of ours.'

'But I've seen the hungry way you kiss her!' Nina accused jealously, stubbornly refusing to believe a single word he said—especially while her foolish heart wanted to open wide and scoop in every claim so it could hold them there as tightly as it could.

'When?' he demanded. 'When have you ever seen me kiss Louisa the way I kiss you?'

Nina shifted restlessly beneath his black flashing gaze. 'When I was hiding in your house that first night,' she admitted guiltily, then lifted her chin to flay him with her eyes. 'She wound herself around you like a serpent, and you were enjoying it!'

Anton let out a rasping sigh. 'The only enjoyment I got from that kiss,' he snapped, 'was the prospect of seeing the back of her as soon as I could! I had just received news about your father's first heart attack, and the last thing I wanted was Louisa making a nuisance of herself with me! I was worried to death about you being alone and vulnerable to that leech Hunter!'

Something began to warm inside her, the first tentative glow of real hope. 'You were lovers,' she accused outright.

'Before I set eyes on you?' His mouth gave a cynical twist. 'There were probably a hundred and one other women before I saw you, Nina,' he said grimly. 'But I cannot remember a single one of them now.'

'You forced me into marrying you,' she charged. 'Bought me—just as you said, like a slave in the marketplace. How can you have done that then claim you love me?'

'Oh, no.' Anton shook his dark head at that one, not for a moment showing any guilt for the way they had married. 'If anyone did any buying, then you bought me, Nina. I sold myself to you—willingly, I do admit—for the price of a sick old man's company that wasn't worth the trouble I have already put into it!'

'What do you mean?' She arched away from him so that she could stare into the dark gravity of his eyes.

'I mean,' he explained, 'that the only real asset Lovell's has is a broken-down old piece of London property which has a conservation order on it that says we cannot touch a single brick or rot-ridden block of wood in it without spending a large fortune renovating it to a strict specification.'

Nina went pale. 'Then all that money you said my father owed you, he—he could never have paid back, even if he hadn't taken ill?'

Anton shook his head. 'Not in our lifetime, no.'

'How——?' She cleared her suddenly dry throat. 'How much altogether did we cost you?'

He told her, and she swayed in his arms. 'Goodness me,' she breathed, 'That certainly is a lot of money.' She was so shocked that she could barely breathe for the minute it took her to take the enormity of it in. 'All these months while I have been thinking myself bought,' she murmured wonderingly, 'when really...' she sent him a curious look '...I got rather a bargain in you, didn't I?'

Blue eyes began to gleam at him, and black went blacker, her smile became a taunt, the tilt of her chin a downright provocation that made him stiffen tensely as he watched in angry wonder the beautiful woman in his arms turn before his eyes into the wickedly wanton creature he had once set free on his island.

And on a rueful grimace he let go of her, taking a step back to eye her sardonically. 'You are never going to let me forget that confession, are you?' he murmured drily.

'Nope,' she said, eyeing him up and down as though he were up for sale all over again. 'Still want me back?' she taunted sweetly.

'God,' he growled, 'come here!' and, with an angry tug, he brought her back into his arms to bruise her mouth with a kiss she more than willingly matched for passion. 'Of course I still want you!' he muttered when he at last managed to slide his mouth away from the clinging heat of hers. 'I cannot remember a moment when I did not want you!'

'Just for my body?' Her fingers made a tantalising sweep across his sensitive nape.

She felt a shiver of pleasure ripple through him. 'For whatever crumb you are willing to throw my way!' he conceded drily. 'As I have just confessed—to my eternal folly, I should imagine—I am your slave for life to do with as you will. I will be content to sit at your feet if that is all you will allow me to do.'

'Liar,' she drawled, using the word to taunt him with the sensual hush of her voice. 'You can't keep your lecherous hands off me, and you know it!'

And while he shook his head in rueful appreciation of that mocking taunt she slipped out of his arms, turning to saunter away, back across his lawn.

'Where are you going?' he demanded bewilderedly.

She spun back to face him, every inch of her so sensually provocative that he almost groaned. 'I'm going inside,' she informed him, then issued her worst provocation yet by waving a lazy hand at him. 'Come on, slave,' she commanded. 'It's cold out here, and I want to—get warm.'

Her blue eyes gleamed a wicked promise at him, and Anton sucked in a deep breath before letting it out again harshly, then, on a husky growl that sent tiny shivers of excitement chasing up and down her spine, he came after her, scooping her up in his arms without even pausing on his way back to the house.

'I will get the better of you yet,' he warned as he carried her into the house and up the wide curving stairway. 'One day, I will win a battle with you, and see how much I taunt you then!'

Nina put her lips to his ear. 'I love you, Anton,' she whispered softly.

It brought him to a shuddering stop outside his bedroom door. 'Have you any idea what it does to me to hear you say that?' he said in a shaken voice.

'Have you any idea what it did to me *not* to hear you say it?'

He looked down into her sombre face, and sighed a little bleakly. 'It was no way to begin, was it? A marriage based on so many lies and deceptions.'

'No,' she agreed, still a little sad as she studied his beautiful, serious face. Then she reached up and placed her lips against his. 'I still loved you despite it all, though.'

His eyes darkened, the black heating with a fire she recognised with a thrill of anticipation. 'Open the door,' he commanded gruffly.

Blue eyes grew wicked all over again. 'What,' she teased, 'this door?'

'Yes, this damned door,' he growled. 'Open it, you tormenting little vixen, or, so help me, I will lay you down right here on the landing and have my lecherous way with you!'

'That sounds interesting,' she mused, the blood beginning to pulse through her veins in delicious triumph at the easy way she could arouse this man.

Then his mouth landed on hers with no warning whatsoever, and she gasped, startled for a moment until that wonderful hot sensual swell began to mushroom inside her, and she gave herself to him without reserve, her pulses racing as she felt his body tremble in response, her fingers scrambling out to find the requested doorhandle.

'Where it all began for me,' she murmured much later when she lay satiated in his arms, glancing around the room she had not entered since that dark mizzly night months ago when her senses had been blasted awake by their mutual pitch-black frenzy of desire.

Anton lifted himself on to an elbow to look at her, a gentle hand going to smooth her tangled hair from her face. 'Then we shall call this a new beginning for both of us,' he suggested tenderly.

'A new beginning.' Nina smiled up at him. 'I like the sound of that.' She reached up to arch an arm around his neck. 'A beginning with no end,' she whispered as she drew his mouth down on to hers.

'Believe it,' Anton said fiercely. 'Because I will never let you go—never!'

On a contented sigh, Nina offered herself up to his hungry demands.

Harlequin Presents®

is

- ☑ exotic
- ☑ dramatic
- ☑ sensual
- ☑ exciting
- ☑ contemporary
- ☑ a fast, involving read
- ☑ terrific!!

*Harlequin Presents—
passionate romances
around the world!*

PRESENTS

HARLEQUIN
Romance®

**HARLEQUIN ROMANCE
IS IN THE
WEDDING BUSINESS...**

The August title in The Bridal Collection is about...
a wedding consultant!

**THE BEST-MADE PLANS
by Leigh Michaels
Harlequin Romance #3214**

THE BRIDAL COLLECTION

THE BRIDE arranged weddings.
The Groom avoided them.
Their own Wedding was ten years late!

Available in July in
The Bridal Collection:
**BOTH OF THEM
by Rebecca Winters**
Harlequin Romance #3210

Available wherever
Harlequin books are sold.

WED-4

WELCOME TO

The quintessential small town where everyone knows everybody else!

Finally, books that capture the pleasure of tuning in to your favorite TV show!

GREAT READING...GREAT SAVINGS...AND A FABULOUS FREE GIFT!

Each book set in Tyler is a self-contained love story; together, the twelve novels stitch the fabric of the community. The covers honor the old American tradition of quilting; each cover depicts a patch of the large Tyler quilt.

With Tyler you can receive a fabulous gift ABSOLUTELY FREE by collecting proofs-of-purchase found in each Tyler book. And use our special Tyler coupons to save on your next TYLER book purchase.

Join your friends at Tyler for the sixth book, SUNSHINE by Pat Warren, available in August.

When Janice Eber becomes a widow, does her husband's friend David provide more than just friendship?

If you missed *Whirlwind* (March), *Bright Hopes* (April), *Wisconsin Wedding* (May), *Monkey Wrench* (June) or *Blazing Star* (July) and would like to order them, send your name, address, zip or postal code, along with a check or money order for $3.99 (please do not send cash), plus 75¢ postage and handling ($1.00 in Canada) for each book ordered, payable to Harlequin Reader Service to:

In the U.S.
3010 Walden Avenue
P.O. Box 1325
Buffalo, NY 14269-1325

In Canada
P.O. Box 609
Fort Erie, Ontario
L2A 5X3

Please specify book title(s) with your order.
Canadian residents add applicable federal and provincial taxes.

TYLER-6

"GET AWAY FROM IT ALL" SWEEPSTAKES

HERE'S HOW THE SWEEPSTAKES WORKS

NO PURCHASE NECESSARY

To enter each drawing, complete the appropriate Official Entry Form or a 3" by 5" index card by hand-printing your name, address and phone number and the trip destination that the entry is being submitted for (i.e., Caneel Bay, Canyon Ranch or London and the English Countryside) and mailing it to: Get Away From It All Sweepstakes, P.O. Box 1397, Buffalo, New York 14269-1397.

No responsibility is assumed for lost, late or misdirected mail. Entries must be sent separately with first class postage affixed, and be received by: 4/15/92 for the Caneel Bay Vacation Drawing, 5/15/92 for the Canyon Ranch Vacation Drawing and 6/15/92 for the London and the English Countryside Vacation Drawing. Sweepstakes is open to residents of the U.S. (except Puerto Rico) and Canada, 21 years of age or older as of 5/31/92.

For complete rules send a self-addressed, stamped (WA residents need not affix return postage) envelope to: Get Away From It All Sweepstakes, P.O. Box 4892, Blair, NE 68009.

© 1992 HARLEQUIN ENTERPRISES LTD.   SWP-RLS

"GET AWAY FROM IT ALL" SWEEPSTAKES

HERE'S HOW THE SWEEPSTAKES WORKS

NO PURCHASE NECESSARY

To enter each drawing, complete the appropriate Official Entry Form or a 3" by 5" index card by hand-printing your name, address and phone number and the trip destination that the entry is being submitted for (i.e., Caneel Bay, Canyon Ranch or London and the English Countryside) and mailing it to: Get Away From It All Sweepstakes, P.O. Box 1397, Buffalo, New York 14269-1397.

No responsibility is assumed for lost, late or misdirected mail. Entries must be sent separately with first class postage affixed, and be received by: 4/15/92 for the Caneel Bay Vacation Drawing, 5/15/92 for the Canyon Ranch Vacation Drawing and 6/15/92 for the London and the English Countryside Vacation Drawing. Sweepstakes is open to residents of the U.S. (except Puerto Rico) and Canada, 21 years of age or older as of 5/31/92.

For complete rules send a self-addressed, stamped (WA residents need not affix return postage) envelope to: Get Away From It All Sweepstakes, P.O. Box 4892, Blair, NE 68009.

© 1992 HARLEQUIN ENTERPRISES LTD.   SWP-RLS

"GET AWAY FROM IT ALL"

Brand-new Subscribers-Only Sweepstakes

OFFICIAL ENTRY FORM

This entry must be received by: June 15, 1992
This month's winner will be notified by: June 30, 1992
Trip must be taken between: July 31, 1992—July 31, 1993

YES, I want to win the vacation for two to England. I understand the prize includes round-trip airfare and the two additional prizes revealed in the BONUS PRIZES insert.

Name _____

Address _____

City _____

State/Prov._____ Zip/Postal Code_____

Daytime phone number _____
(Area Code)

Return entries with invoice in envelope provided. Each book in this shipment has two entry coupons — and the more coupons you enter, the better your chances of winning!
© 1992 HARLEQUIN ENTERPRISES LTD.   3M-CPN

"GET AWAY FROM IT ALL"

Brand-new Subscribers-Only Sweepstakes

OFFICIAL ENTRY FORM

This entry must be received by: June 15, 1992
This month's winner will be notified by: June 30, 1992
Trip must be taken between: July 31, 1992—July 31, 1993

YES, I want to win the vacation for two to England. I understand the prize includes round-trip airfare and the two additional prizes revealed in the BONUS PRIZES insert.

Name _____

Address _____

City _____

State/Prov._____ Zip/Postal Code_____

Daytime phone number _____
(Area Code)

Return entries with invoice in envelope provided. Each book in this shipment has two entry coupons — and the more coupons you enter, the better your chances of winning!
© 1992 HARLEQUIN ENTERPRISES LTD.   3M-CPN